Charles H. Stowell

A primer of health for primary classes

With special reference to the effects of alcoholic drinks and tobacco upon the

human system

Charles H. Stowell

A primer of health for primary classes
With special reference to the effects of alcoholic drinks and tobacco upon the human system

ISBN/EAN: 9783742832887

Manufactured in Europe, USA, Canada, Australia, Japa

Cover: Foto ©Andreas Hilbeck / pixelio.de

Manufactured and distributed by brebook publishing software (www.brebook.com)

Charles H. Stowell

A primer of health for primary classes

A

PRIMER OF HEALTH

for Primary Classes

WITH SPECIAL REFERENCE
TO THE EFFECTS OF ALCOHOLIC DRINKS AND TOBACCO
UPON THE HUMAN SYSTEM

By CHARLES H. STOWELL, M.D.

LATE PROFESSOR OF HISTOLOGY AND MICROSCOPY, AND ASSISTANT PROFESSOR
OF PHYSIOLOGY, UNIVERSITY OF MICHIGAN.
AUTHOR OF STUDENT'S MANUAL OF HISTOLOGY; MICROSCOPICAL DIAGNOSIS; THE STRUCTURE OF
TEETH; A HEALTHY BODY; THE ESSENTIALS OF HEALTH, ETC.
LATE EDITOR OF "THE MICROSCOPE"; EDITOR OF "THE NATIONAL
MEDICAL REVIEW."

FULLY ILLUSTRATED

WITH ORIGINAL SKETCHES BY THE AUTHOR

SILVER, BURDETT & COMPANY
NEW YORK ... BOSTON ... CHICAGO
1894

PRESSWORK BY BERWICK & SMITH,
BOSTON, U.S.A.

PREFACE.

THIS work is designed as a pupil's book for use in the primary grades of schools, both public and private. It is so written that the subject-matter can be read and understood by pupils who are able to read well in the ordinary Second Reader.

While stating in simple language some elementary facts in anatomy and physiology, especial attention has been given to rules for the preservation of health.

A careful search for the cause of the physical ills of adult life reveals the fact that much of the suffering is the result of repeated violations of hygienic laws early in life. It is no mitigation of these ills that the laws are violated through ignorance; but the fact that most of the violations occur from lack of knowledge furnishes a potent reason for training the young with great care.

The mental and moral degeneracy of some of our young men can easily be traced to the early use of the cigarette and the light alcoholic drinks. If the coming generation is to be strong physically, mentally, and morally, our young people must learn to avoid the use of both tobacco and alcohol.

That alcoholic beverages produce the most disastrous effects on individuals and communities is fairly well understood, but the evils of the tobacco habit are greatly underrated. Tobacco is a positive and most deadly poison to the young boy. It may not deprive him of his life, but the testimony is abundant and conclusive that it can warp and dwarf his mental and moral endowments. No boy who uses tobacco can hope to develop into a full and perfect manhood.

By earnestly presenting the simple truths as laid down in the text of this little book, teachers can exert an influence for good which will be both valuable and permanent. The reward of such effort will be the highest, the development of a wiser, more temperate, and more moral people.

CHARLES H. STOWELL.

WASHINGTON, D. C., May, 1892.

CONTENTS.

A PRIMER OF HEALTH.

CHAPTER I

WHY WE EAT.

THE boys and girls who read this book are growing very fast. Only a few years ago they were quite small; yet we know that each year to come they expect to be much larger and stronger than they are now.

What is it makes you grow so fast? Is it the air you breathe? No, not entirely; because you would soon starve if you had only the air. Is it the water you drink? No; although water is necessary, yet you could not live on that alone. Let us study some of the plants, to see if we can find what it is that makes them grow.

Can you tell why it is that a small, young tree in a few years will grow large

enough for you to climb? Would it grow
if you should pull it up and place it on the
floor in the house? Its branches would
never be strong enough for you to fasten
a swing around them, would they? Do
you think the plants in the flower garden
would give you their beautiful flowers if
you should pull them up by the roots?
No, indeed; they would soon lose their
leaves and blossoms if they were so badly
treated.

We know that the trees and plants need
something more than fresh air, water, and
sunlight. They will surely die unless they
are fastened to the soil in some way. How
are they fastened to the soil?

Have you not often noticed how many
roots there are to trees and plants? The
large roots, with their little branches, go
down deep into the earth and take from it
something necessary to the life of the leaves
and flowers above the ground. What do
the little roots find? Food. What makes
the trees and flowers grow? Food. What

makes boys and girls grow to be strong men and women? Food.

THE PLANTS TAKE THEIR FOOD AS THEY FIND IT.

Do you think it makes any difference what kind of food is used? Yes, you believe it must make a difference, because you have noticed some things about plants. Tell us, what is it you have seen? Well, you say, one person always has his plants looking fresh and thrifty, while his next-door neighbor never has any luck with flowers. You are right when you tell us that one person knows what kind of food to give his plants, while the other does not. One knows what soil is best for certain plants, as well as how much sunlight and water are needed.

Do you think the dark, damp soil looks anything like the beautiful white rose? Yet in some way the roots of the rose-bush take food from the earth and change it, so that the leaves are made to grow, and the flowers to bloom.

You do not think your own body looks much like the food you eat, do you? Yet we know that our food becomes changed, in some way, into all the different parts of the body.

We have been telling how the food makes the body grow; but it does more. Just think a moment. A full-grown person is never any taller, and he may never be more fleshy, yet he eats heartily three times each day. Why does he eat this food if he does not grow?

We will let you answer this question after we ask another. While you were waiting at the depot, did you ever see an engine as it stands, puffing, puffing? No-

tice how the engineer oils the joints and
polishes the brass trimmings. Yet, sooner
or later, this great machine will wear out.
It began to wear the very first time it
moved; and now, every little while, the
engineer is obliged to take away some
badly worn piece and put a new one in its
place. The engine wears out, and has to
be repaired.

It is so with our bodies; they are constantly wearing out. Every slight motion
of the body causes a small amount of wear;
while such active work as running and
jumping causes the body to wear out much
faster.

Some one asks, If this be true, why do
we not all waste away? Because the body
is repaired. The food we eat is changed
into the parts of the body that are wearing
out. In answer to our question, Why do
we eat? you are now ready to answer: Because the food keeps the body in repair, so
that it will not waste away, and because it
makes the bodies of young people grow.

The boys and girls for us are those who, as they grow larger and older in body, grow purer and truer in heart.

" I am looking for boys that are strong and true,
Boys that have courage to dare and do.
Does that mean you? and you? and you?

" I am looking for girls that are strong and true,
Girls that have courage to dare and do.
Does that mean you? and you? and you?"

QUESTIONS.

1. Are you growing very fast?
2. Does the air alone make you grow?
3. Is it the water you drink?
4. Would a tree grow if placed on the floor?
5. If you pull plants up by the roots, what happens?
6. Name three things plants need.
7. Are these all?
8. What more is necessary?
9. How are they fastened to the soil?
10. What do the roots find?
11. Why do some plants look fresher than others?
12. Into what is our food changed?
13. What is said about a steam engine?
14. What keeps our bodies from wasting away?
15. Give two reasons why we need to eat.
16. Can you repeat the verses on this page?

CHAPTER II.

FOODS WE SHOULD EAT.

IF food becomes changed into our own bodies, do you not think we should be very careful what we eat? Now the best foods are not always the most expensive; indeed, some of them are the cheapest.

What is one of the best foods? You all know the answer: milk. A better food cannot be imagined. Children live on it for years, and many grown people use it freely. It is a much better food for young people than meat; and it is a far better drink than tea or coffee. We wish every boy and girl could have a large glass of it three times a day.

Can you think of another food that is used very generally? A food nearly as valuable as milk? Yes, indeed; bread and butter. Eggs are valuable, only they should not be cooked too hard. Beefsteak is the best meat. It should be broiled and served rare. Mutton is also a good food, but veal and pork are not so good.

Is it best to eat much fruit? Nearly all the fruits are useful. They are pleasant to the taste, and they give an appetite for other foods. But you should always be careful not to eat either unripe or over-ripe fruit. There are some things of which you should eat very sparingly. You may guess the names of some of them, — rich cakes and pies, heavy, rich puddings, hot bread, and pork.

Did you ever hear of a boy or girl who did not like candy? It really seems that the desire for sweet things is a natural one. For this reason, a proper amount of sugar should be used in the food. Ripe apples, peaches, grapes, and oranges are sweet, because they contain sugar. But if you do not have enough sugar in your food and in the fruit you eat, and you still desire something sweet, then you can make some home-made candy. You should remember, however, that if you eat too much sugar, you may disturb the stomach and take away the appetite for good food.

Do you know of anything that tastes better, when you are thirsty, than a glass of pure, cool water? Did you know that a person will die sooner without water than he will without food? What should we do without water? How eagerly the horse and the dog drink it! Notice how the birds bathe in it! Even the plants love it, for no matter how their leaves may droop in the hot sun, the evening dew or the brisk shower brings back to them all their freshness and beauty.

About three-fourths of the weight of the body is water; so that if you weigh eighty pounds, nearly sixty pounds of it will be water. Now, when it forms so large a part of the body, it certainly must be very important that only the purest and the best of water be used.

We take a large amount of water with our food, but not enough to satisfy the

thirst. We are obliged to take a great deal of water as drink. Yet we should never take iced water with our meals. It weakens the stomach and often causes illness. It is a

dangerous practice to drink a glass of ice-
cold water when the body is overheated.
Remember that cool water quenches the
thirst better than ice-water, and that there
is no danger in its moderate use.

How many of you live in the country, or
have been there on a visit, and have seen
the cows and sheep come hurrying to
answer the farmer's call, hoping he may
have some salt for them? Watch how
eagerly they eat it! It must be that these
animals need the salt, or they would not be
so anxious for it. We, too, need salt with
our food. We would soon tire of many
articles of food if no salt were added to
them.

Have you ever noticed how hard bone is?
What makes it so much harder than the
flesh around it? Because it is made largely
of lime. When the body is growing, the
bones must be fed with lime. Where can
you get this lime? You do not add it to
the food as salt is added, and yet you must
have a great deal of it. This is the way it

is obtained. The growing grass and the grain take the lime from the soil. How do you get it from the grass? The cows eat the grass and change some of it into milk, and when you drink the milk you get the lime. How do you obtain the lime from the grains? By grinding the wheat into flour and making the flour into bread.

When there is not enough lime in the body the bones are soft and easily bent. The teeth also are soft and very liable to decay. Therefore, when the body is young and growing rapidly it should be supplied with plenty of this substance. We have now given you another reason why bread and milk are so useful for young people.

QUESTIONS.

1. Name one of the best foods.
2. Name some other good foods.
3. What is said about eating fruit?
4. Is water an important food?
5. Tell some things said about drinking water.
6. Do we need salt in our food?
7. How do we obtain lime for a food?

CHAPTER III.

HOW WE DIGEST OUR FOOD.

LET us sit down together for a good dinner. We will begin the meal with some peaches, oranges, or grapes, because fruit is best if eaten before the meal. The juices of these fruits will help to quench our thirst, and will give us an appetite for the good things coming.

Now, what meat will you take? We have beef and mutton. You can have eggs, if you prefer. We have no pork, because if used at all, it should be used only by those who work hard and are very strong and hearty. You can have the beef or mutton either broiled or roasted. We do not fry them, because frying makes them so hard and greasy.

What vegetables will you have? There is a long list from which we might choose, but we will be satisfied to give you some

potatoes, thoroughly cooked; tomatoes, raw
or cooked; and some rice that has been
cooked a long time until it is very soft.

Would you like some hot bread? Well,
you cannot get it at our table, because,
when fresh and hot, it often causes trouble
with the stomach. But eat heartily of
our cold bread and fresh butter. It is a
valuable food, and very pleasant to the
taste.

Just a little salt, did you say? Yes, a
trifle, — enough to give a good flavor to
the food. Not any pepper, or at least
you must be satisfied with very, very little.
Too many spices, as pepper, cloves, and
cinnamon, are not good for the stomach.

What will you have to quench your
thirst? Hot tea or coffee? Iced tea or
cold lemonade? No, indeed, none of these;
for very hot and very cold drinks, especially
at meal-time, are injurious. Then, too, neither tea nor coffee is good for the growing body. So we will bring you a glass of
cool water and another glass of milk; or if

you prefer, you can take the second glass of milk in place of the meat.

Are you already anxious for your dessert? We fear you will be disappointed, for all we have is some boiled custard. Some days we have light puddings, but we do not believe much in rich pastries.

There are other good articles of food, as oysters, chicken, turkey, celery, and cooked fruits. But pork, sausage, salt meats, lobsters, cucumbers, and pickles we would rather not pass to you.

Now that our dinner is ready, let us begin to eat slowly and chat pleasantly. As soon as you place some solid food in the mouth and begin to chew, notice what happens! The mouth becomes filled with a juice which moistens and mixes with the food so that it can be swallowed easily. This juice is called the saliva.

Why did you chew the solid food? Why not swallow it in large pieces instead of crushing and grinding it with the teeth? Because the solid food must be in small pieces when it reaches the stomach, or there is danger that the stomach will not do its work well. One of the most common causes of stomach trouble is that the food is not chewed as fine as it should be.

Can you tell how many teeth there are in the first set? Just ten in each jaw. But at

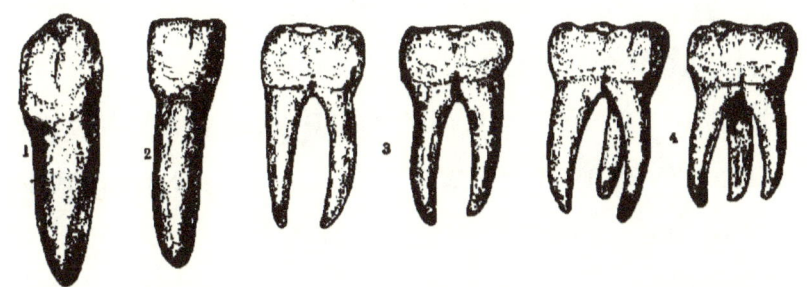

Fig. 4. Teeth from the second or permanent set. 1, a front tooth; 2, an eye-tooth; 3, back teeth from the lower jaw; 4, back teeth from the upper jaw.

five or six years of age these begin to fall out, or are pulled, and the second set appears. When we have all the teeth of the second set, there are sixteen in each jaw. Some of the teeth, as the front teeth, are sharp for cutting, while others, as the back teeth, are for grinding and crushing.

Did you ever have a tooth pulled, or suffer from the toothache? Not very much sport, was it? We should try to keep our second teeth with us all our lives. A few simple rules may aid us in doing this:—

1. Do not crack nuts between the teeth.

2. Do not pick them with any hard substance, as a pin.

3. Clean them with a soft brush, at least once each day.

4. As soon as a cavity appears, or if a tooth aches, consult a dentist.

If the bread you are eating is a little dry, do not wash it down with a large quantity of water. Eat more slowly and take but little water. A single glass of water should be enough for any one meal. If that is not enough drink for the warmest weather, then you would better quench the thirst before going to the table, rather than wait until seated and then drink too much with the food.

What follows after chewing the food? It is swallowed, is it not? You never thought there was anything very curious about swallowing, did you? But there is something about it both curious and wonderful. You know there are two passages down the throat. Through one of these the air reaches the lungs. This passage you can feel at the front of the throat. It is called the windpipe. The other is farther back and is for the food to pass into the stomach.

Now, why does not the food go down the windpipe and choke us? Because there is, over the top of the windpipe, a little lid. This lid opens when we breathe, and shuts down tightly when we swallow. Sometimes the lid does not shut quite quick enough, and we are choked. You say you have swallowed something the wrong way. But this rarely happens. This little lid works so nicely that, when we swallow, the food goes directly down into the stomach.

———•———

"But more than all, I would be good,
 Sincere, and pure, and true;
 And as I eat my daily food,
 Grow wiser, — would n't you?"

CHAPTER IV.

MORE ABOUT DIGESTION.

How do you suppose the stomach can take the solid food you had with your dinner and change it, so that it will mix with the blood? First of all, the solid food will have to be softened, or dissolved, will it not? If it can be made as soft and thin as water, then it could surely mix with the blood.

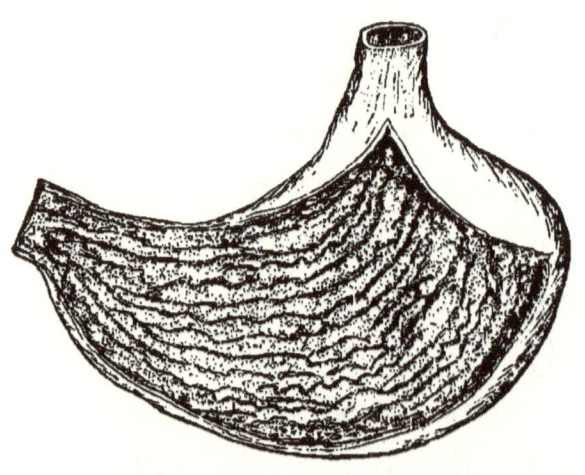

FIG. 5. The stomach. The front walls have been removed to show the lining membrane which makes the gastric juice.

Now that is just what the stomach is for. It dissolves the foods. How does it do this? By means of a juice, called the gastric juice. As soon as the food reaches

the stomach it mixes with this juice which
the stomach makes. It is a very powerful juice, for it dissolves the foods, and
changes them,
so that they can
mix with the
blood. This
softening and
changing of the
food is called di-
gestion.

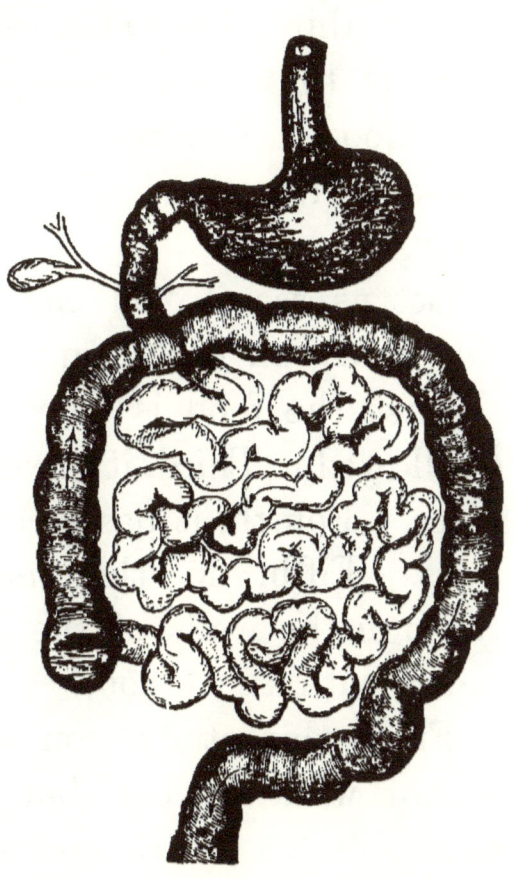

After the food
has been digest-
ed in the stom-
ach it passes out
into the intes-
tines, where it
meets with other
juices. If you
will look at Fig.
6, you will see

Fig. 6. (1) The stomach. Below this are
the intestines.

that the intestine is a long tube which is
so coiled that it takes but little room.

How do you suppose the digested food

passes from the intestines into the blood? In this way: In the walls of the intestines are many blood vessels; and the food, which is now thin like water, soaks through the walls of these blood vessels and mixes with the blood. You will soon learn how the blood carries the food to all parts of the body.

Let us see if you can give a review of this study on digestion:—

First, the food is chewed. Second, it is swallowed. Third, it mixes with the gastric juice. Fourth, it passes out into the intestines. Fifth, in the intestines it soaks through the walls of the blood vessels and mixes with the blood.

From this study you can learn that it is not what we eat, but what we digest, that gives us health and strength. Young people are generally so healthy that they pay little attention to what they eat or drink. But they will not always enjoy this health if they repeatedly break certain laws.

Do you think you could keep well if you should work all the time and never stop for rest? Then how can you expect your stomach to keep strong if you make it work constantly, as it must if you eat between meals?

Do not eat between meals.

Do not eat in a hurry.

Do not eat too rich food.

Do not eat just before going to bed.

Do not drink iced water nor iced tea with your meals.

Do not drink or eat anything that has in it wine or any form of alcohol.

Do not be fretful and cross. To a good appetite and perfect digestion, add cheerfulness, and a pleasant word for all.

QUESTIONS.

1. What is the stomach for?
2. What does the gastric juice do?
3. How does the digested food pass into the blood?
4. Give a review of the study on digestion?
5. What can you learn from this study?
6. Should you work all the time and never rest?
7. Ought your stomach to have rest also?
8. What does the lesson say you should not do?

CHAPTER V.

IS ALCOHOL A FOOD?

WE have learned that if we wish to keep strong, the stomach must do its work well.

But there are many things that harm the stomach. Eating unripe fruit, and too much rich food, often cause pain and severe stomach trouble. In fact, we have known persons to be very ill from drinking iced water when they were over-heated. Most of you are probably very fond of ice cream, yet if you eat too heartily of it you may suffer severely. These facts teach us that we must be temperate in all things.

Now there is one kind of drink which is not good for the stomach. It makes the inside of the stomach red, or inflamed, and the gastric juice cannot digest the food as it should. What is this drink? We call it strong drink. By strong drink, we mean any drink containing alcohol, as cider, wine, whiskey, brandy, and beer.

Some people never take enough wine to get intoxicated, but they drink a glass or two with each meal. If we should ask one of them why he does so, he would probably reply that he drank it to help his stomach digest the food. He may have some trouble with his stomach, and thinks the strong drink will help him. What a great mistake is this! If such people would throw away all kinds of drink containing alcohol, eat plain, simple food only, and live rightly in other ways, it is probable the trouble with their stomachs would soon pass away.

Remember how the food you take into the stomach at last mixes with the blood, and is carried to all parts of the body. So it would be if you should put .beer or wine into the stomach; it would soon mix with the blood and be carried all over the body.

But some persons say alcohol is a food. What do you think about it? If you were hungry, would you rather have it than milk? Do you think your body would grow, and keep strong and well if you should use it, instead of bread and meat? No, indeed. There is nothing in any of the strong drinks equal to the meats and vegetables which are used as foods. We know that alcohol is not a food.

Then is it good to quench the thirst? No, because one drink of it has the power to make us desire another.

But some boy says he has noticed that the men who sell beer, and who probably drink a good deal of it themselves, are almost always very fleshy. Now, he says, if it makes men fleshy, is it not a good food? We answer, No; because it is not fat that makes a man strong; it is muscle. Very fleshy persons are not usually so well as those who are not so fleshy. Strong persons try, by exercise and hard training, to get rid of their fat, and make their muscles hard. Now what is the trouble with the man who is made fleshy by drinking beer?

His muscles are changing to fat, and he is not strong. There is so much fat that he cannot exercise well, and his stomach gets out of order. His heart grows weak, because there is fat in its walls. He gets out of breath easily, and suffers much from a diseased heart.

Now which do you prefer, — sound, hard muscles or soft, fatty muscles? A healthy heart or a fatty, diseased heart? Strong muscles and a sound heart are not often found in a body made fleshy by drinking beer.

Look at Fig. 13 and see what a large organ is the liver. It is called an organ, because it has some special work to do. For this reason we call the eye the organ of sight, and the ear the organ of hearing. Now the work of the liver is very important. If it does not do its work well, the whole body is made to suffer. Yet you must remember that the liver is one of the first parts of the body to be injured by the use of strong drink.

Can you tell us how we may all escape the bad effects of strong drink? Only one sure way. *Never take the first glass.*

TOBACCO AND DIGESTION.

A great many persons say they are obliged to smoke after eating, for if they do not, they fear they will have some trouble with their stomachs. This is a very weak excuse, for the use of the tobacco itself often disturbs the digestion of the food. So smoking only makes a bad matter worse. A much better thing for these persons would be to stop using tobacco altogether. But we can give better advice than this, and so can you. What is it? *Never begin to use tobacco.*

TEA AND COFFEE.

If boys and girls expect to keep in sound health, they must not form the habit of using tea or coffee. Nothing can take the place of cool water and pure milk.

CHAPTER VI.

THE BLOOD.

WERE you ever out in the woods where they make maple sugar? If so, you know that a small hole is bored into the maple-tree, and from this there flows a clear fluid, which is called sap. This does not flow in a large stream, but only drop by drop. Now this sap is on its way from the tender roots of the tree to the little branches and leaves far above; it contains the food which makes the tree grow larger and taller.

Some time when you walk out into the country, see if you can find a plant called the milkweed; if so, break a large stem of it and notice what a thick, white juice comes from the end. This juice contains the food which makes the plant grow. Suppose you prick the end of your finger with a needle, what happens? A fluid appears, does it not? This fluid is not clear, like the sap of the maple, nor white, like the juice of the milkweed, but it has a bright red color. What is the name of it? Blood.

The blood contains the food that repairs the body and makes it grow. Do you think

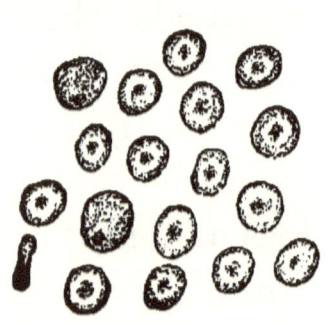

FIG. 7. Human blood, as seen with a microscope.

you could cut through the skin anywhere without causing the blood to flow? No, indeed, for it is freely distributed throughout the body. But there are a few places, as the hair, the nails, and the outer part of the skin, in which there is no blood.

The blood would look clear like water were it not for some very minute bodies. These little bodies are flat and round, yet so small that thousands and thousands of them could be placed side by side on the head of a pin. We know there are many millions of them in a single drop of blood. We often compare these little bodies to tiny boats floating in the blood, carrying what is needed from one part of the body to another. The color of these bodies is what gives the color to the blood. In Fig. 7 you can see how they look. Sometimes they make the blood appear a bright red color. Then again they make it much darker, nearly a purple color.

Did you ever cut your finger so the blood flowed from it freely? If the cut was not very bad, the blood stopped flowing of its own accord, did it not? Now what made the blood stop flowing? Why did it not keep running, as it did at first? Because the blood that is on the outside of the vessels becomes thick and thus stops up the openings in the blood vessels. We say the blood clots. Think how often the lower animals would bleed to death from their injuries were it not for this clotting of the blood!

Whenever the body is wounded in any way, the clotting of the blood can be aided by keeping quiet, and by pressing on the wounded spot. Sometimes such large vessels are cut that it is necessary to call a surgeon.

Have you ever noticed how pale some persons are when in poor health? Their blood is not as red as it should be, or perhaps there is not enough of it. We are always glad to see the red cheeks of the boys and girls when they come in from play. But how sad we feel when their pale faces show they are not in good health. Remember this motto:—

> GOOD FOOD HELPS TO MAKE GOOD BLOOD.

QUESTIONS.

1. How is sap obtained?
2. What does it contain?
3. Tell something about the milkweed.
4. Is the blood clear like the sap of the maple?
5. What color is it?
6. What does the blood contain?
7. Are there very many of these little bodies?
8. To what do we compare them?
9. What makes the blood stop flowing from a cut or wound?
10. How can we aid the clotting of the blood?

CHAPTER VII.

THE HEART AND THE BLOOD VESSELS.

WERE you ever at a fire, and did you watch the engine as it sent the water through a tube to some distant building? What sends the water with such force against the burning building? You answer: " Why, the engine."

Now we will ask you what sends the blood to all parts of the body. You answer: " It must

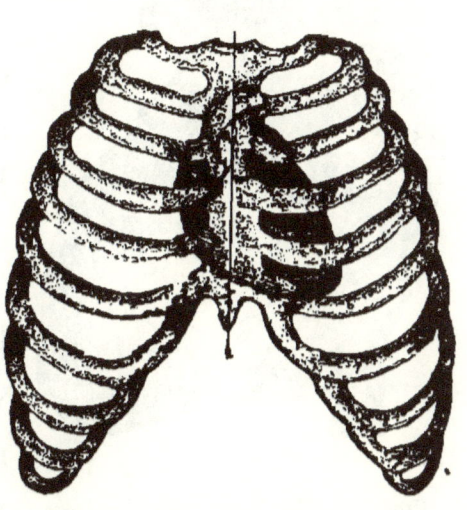

FIG. 8.   The position of the heart.

be some great or powerful engine." Yes, and the name of this engine is the heart.

You can sometimes feel the beating of this engine by placing the hand over the left side of the chest.

The heart is a large hollow muscle. It is situated in the chest with the lungs. If you look at Fig. 8, you will have a good idea of the location of the heart. Did you know before that a good deal of the heart is directly beneath the breast-bone? Some of it, even, is to the right of that bone; but the point of the heart is well over on the left side.

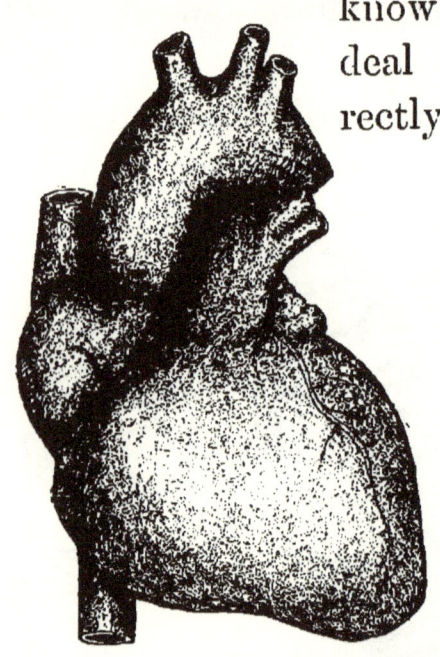

FIG. 9. The heart, and the large blood vessels at its upper part.

Although the heart does so much work, yet it is not much larger than your closed fist. It is shaped somewhat like a pear, with the small end down and to the left. The shape is well shown in Fig. 9. This figure also shows the large blood vessels through which the blood flows to and from the heart.

We said the heart is hollow, but there is within it more than one cavity. In the first place a firm wall, or partition, divides the heart into two parts, making the right side and the left side of the heart. This wall is so complete that not a particle of blood can go directly from one side of the heart to the other.

One of these days, you may learn how the large cavity on each side of the heart is divided into two cavities, so that really there are four

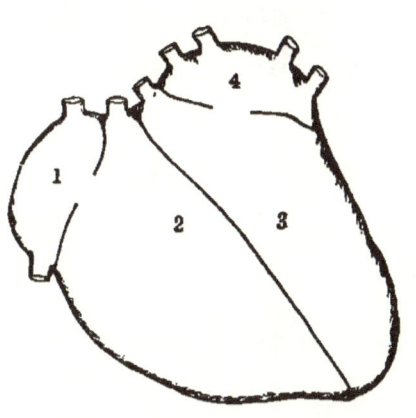

FIG. 10.   This illustrates the firm wall which divides the heart into two parts. The wall is shown by the line between the figures 2 and 3; 1 and 2 make the right side of the heart, 3 and 4 the left side.

cavities in the heart, two for each side. But we will only ask you to remember now that there are two sides to the heart, and that the blood cannot go directly from one side to the other.

Yes, there is just one thing more we will ask you to remember. The right side of the heart always contains the dark blood; and the left side, the bright red blood.

Let us look at the fire engine again. How does the water get into the engine? By means of a pipe, which is fastened to the hydrant or placed in a cistern. How does the water leave the engine? By means of another pipe. Now you can tell us how the blood enters the engine of our bodies, the heart, and how it leaves again. It is by means of soft tubes, or pipes, called the blood vessels.

The blood vessels carrying the blood *to* the heart are called veins, and those carrying the blood *from* the heart are called arteries. The arteries carry the bright blood, and the veins, the dark blood. The bright blood in the arteries is the purest and best.

Are all the blood vessels of the same size? Most certainly not. Those nearest the heart are very large; but as we examine the vessels farther and farther from the heart, we notice that they become smaller and smaller. Fig. 11 shows how one large artery starts from the heart, H, then, bending upon itself, goes down the body by the side of the backbone. Notice, too, how it gives off many branches on its way. Some of these go to the head (1), carrying food to the brain; others go to the arms (2), taking food to the muscles; while other large branches (3) go to the lower limbs. Now just imagine how, in this way, great numbers of little branches carry food to all parts of the body.

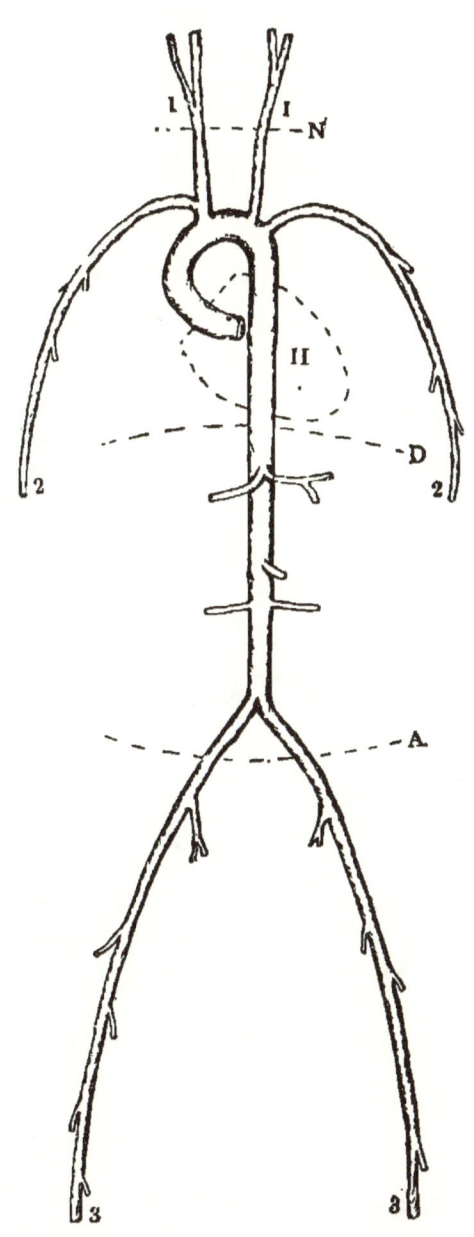

Fig. 11. H, the heart; N, the neck; D, the lower part of the chest; A, the hips. The large blood vessels carry blood to the following parts: 1, to the head; 2, to the arms; 3, to the lower limbs.

Have you ever been so ill that a physician came to see you? And did he place his fingers on the thumb side of your wrist "to feel the pulse"? What was this for? Because the doctor wished to know how many times a minute the heart was beat-

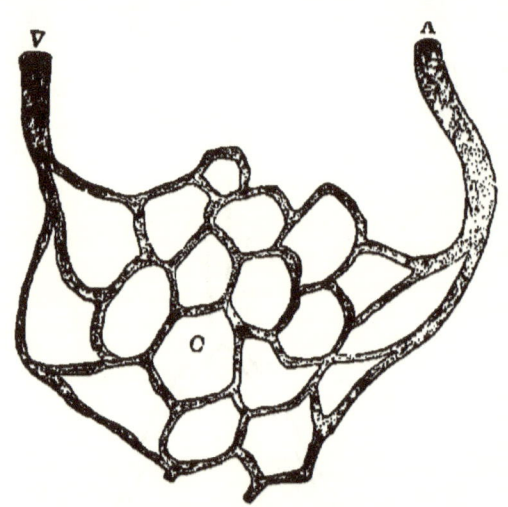

ing. Each time the heart beats it sends out some blood into the arteries, and this makes them swell out, or throb. All of the arteries throb in this way. You can very easily feel one throb,

FIG. 12. A, a small artery ; c, small blood vessels (called capillaries), very much enlarged ; v, a small vein.

by gently pressing the fingers over the side of the neck.

Look at Fig. 12 and notice how many times the artery, A, divides. It divides again and again until there is a perfect network of fine blood vessels, as shown at c.

Notice, too, how these small blood vessels come together again until quite a large vein, at v, is formed. From this we learn that there is a fine network of small blood vessels throughout the body. The little blood vessels are so close together that it is impossible to prick through the skin with the finest needle without wounding some of them and making the blood flow.

Are you ready now to give us a brief review of this lesson? First of all there is a little engine which we call the heart. When this is filled with blood it suddenly becomes smaller, pushing the bright blood through the arteries. This makes the arteries throb, or pulsate. The arteries take the blood to the veins, and the veins take it directly back to the heart.

QUESTIONS.

1. What sends the blood to all parts of the body?
2. Give the location of the heart.
3. What is said about its size and shape?
4. Tell about the cavities within the heart.
5. Where do we find the dark blood? The bright blood?
6. What blood vessels are called veins?
7. What blood vessels carry blood *from* the heart?
8. Give a review of this lesson.

CHAPTER VIII.

ALCOHOL, TOBACCO, AND THE HEART.

Do you think you can control the beating of your heart? Suppose you sit down quietly and try it. Command your heart to beat very fast, and then command it to beat slower. It will not obey you; it beats on as steadily as the tick of the old clock. No matter whether we are sound asleep or wide awake, it still keeps steadily at work. Why does it not beat fast one minute and then very slow the next? What makes it keep beating away just so many times each minute? You say there must be something controlling the heart. Yes, it is controlled by some little white, thread-like fibers which we call the nerves. If these nerves should lose their control over the heart, it would beat faster. Would any harm come from this? Most certainly, for if the heart beats faster than necessary, it does so much extra work, and this often causes it to become diseased.

Now, it is a fact that strong drink, or the alcoholic liquors, affect these nerves so that they lose their complete power over the heart. What is the result of this? The heart beats faster.

Tell us which you think would be the easier: to walk or to run for a whole hour? You answer, "Of course it is less tiresome to walk." So it is less tiresome for the heart to beat a certain number of times each minute than to beat much faster.

From this we learn that one effect of alcoholic liquors is to make the heart beat faster; and if this be long continued, it often causes disease of the heart.

Do you remember what we said about beer making some people fleshy? We said that the muscles become soft and filled with fat. Because the heart is a muscle, it, too, may become fatty from drinking beer. This makes it larger, and at the same time softer and weaker. Physicians call this discase "the fatty heart," because there is so much fat in the muscle of the heart. At last the heart is so weak it cannot do its work, and suddenly death occurs.

From this we learn that some alcoholic drinks may cause a disease of the heart which no physician can cure, and which may result in sudden death.

Did you ever see a man who had used a great deal of strong drink for a number of years? If so, you probably noticed that he had red eyes, red cheeks, and a red nose. What does this show? That there is trouble with the blood vessels of these parts. There is too much blood in them. This alone proves the great power of alcohol to injure the body.

.Is there no escape from the terrible effects of strong drink? Yes, there is always one easy way of escape. Try it. *Never take the first glass.*

Have you ever run or played so hard that you could scarcely get your breath? If so, did you notice that your heart beat very fast and hard? Almost painful, was it not? Sometimes the heart will beat in this way when we are greatly frightened. This rapid and violent beating of the heart is called palpitation.

Boys can easily have this palpitation of the heart, if they want it. They need not be frightened in order to have it, neither will they be obliged to run very hard. All they need to do, if they desire it and the severe pain that sometimes goes with it, will be to smoke cigarettes.

Boys who smoke cigarettes often have these sudden attacks of rapid and violent action of the heart. The heart beats very fast, then slower, then faster again. There is sometimes a faint and sickening feeling, with sharp pain in the left side. The doctors call this an "irritable heart," or a "tobacco heart." It may lead to very serious results.

No boy can smoke cigarettes or use tobacco in any form and expect to become a strong, healthy man.

4

CHAPTER IX.

BREATHING.

WHERE did you say we could find the bright red blood? Oh, yes, in the arteries. The arteries carry the bright blood to every part of the body. The blood gives up its food, as it flows along, to the parts that need it; and it takes in exchange the materials that are no longer useful. How does this blood flow back to the heart? Through the veins, does it not? But the blood in the veins is no longer of a bright red color; it is nearly a dark purple. Now the heart does not send this dark, impure blood through the body, but to the lungs. Here in the lungs the dark, impure blood is changed to bright, pure blood again. If the lungs do all this work they must be very important. Let us study them carefully.

There are two lungs, one in each side of the chest. The outside of a lung is very smooth, so that it can move easily against the walls of the chest; but the inside is full of holes, making it look somewhat like a sponge.

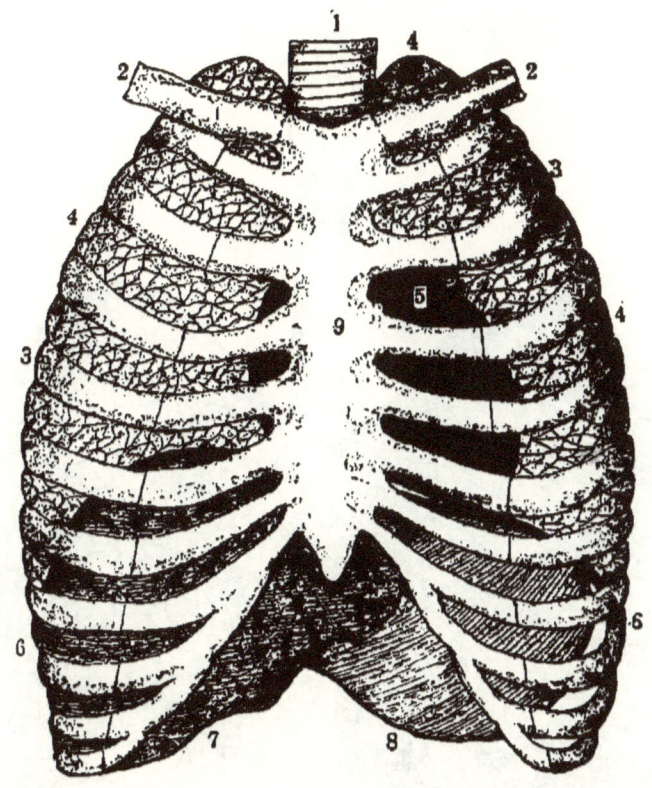

FIG. 13. The position of the lungs, and other organs near them. 1, the windpipe; 2, the collar bone; 3, the ribs; 4, the lungs; 5, the heart; 6, the dark, curved line which forms the lower part of the chest (it is the same as shown at D, Fig. 11); 7, the liver; 8, the stomach; 9, the breastbone.

You may think of a lung as made of a number of little sacs. These sacs are very elastic, as if they were rubber. They will swell out, or expand, as they do when we breathe in the air; then they will become smaller, or contract, and push out the air.

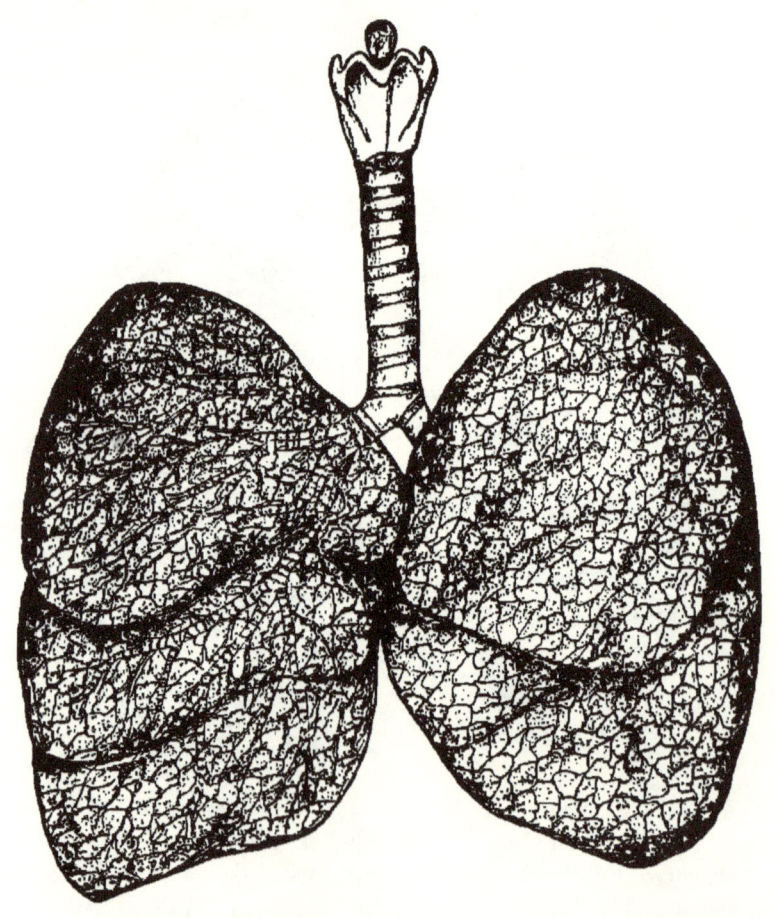

Fig. 14. The lungs; and the windpipe, which carries the air from the throat to the lungs.

Suppose you take in a good full breath of air; see how your chest swells! Each little air sac becomes filled with air, making the lungs larger. Now breathe out the air, and notice how the walls of the chest fall in. The little air sacs have contracted and pushed the air out.

What is all this for? Do you think the air you breathe out of your lungs is just the same as the air you breathe in? No, indeed. Many things happened to the air when it was in the little air sacs.

First of all, let us tell you that there are many blood vessels in the lungs; they almost cover the walls of each of the little air sacs. In breathing, the air comes so close to these blood vessels, that only the thinnest wall is between the air and the blood.

Now look at the back of your hand, or at your wrist. Can you see any of the blue lines, called veins? In some persons they do not show, while in others they show clearly, and look very blue. Do you think these veins hold a blue fluid? It certainly looks so. But the blood is not quite blue.

It is more nearly a dark purple; it certainly
is not a bright red. Now, when you prick
your finger, the blood looks red, does it
not? What has changed it from a dark
color to a bright red·? The air. Just as
soon as the air touched the blood, it made
it brighter.

Does the air ever get very near the blood
while the blood is in the body? Oh, yes.
We just told you that in the lungs the air
and the blood come very close together.
Does the air in the lungs change the color
of the blood? Yes, indeed. Some of the
air mixes with the blood and quickly
changes its dark color to a bright red.

From this we learn that the blood obtains
fresh air in the lungs. Does it give anything in exchange for this air? Yes. It
gives up many impurities gathered from all
parts of the body.

When we breathe out the air, these impurities escape. If all this be true, do you
think we should breathe the same air over
and over again?

We will now review the lesson. Give two changes that occur in the blood when it is in the lungs. First, it obtains a supply of fresh air which changes its color; and second, many impurities escape from it. After the blood is thus purified, where does it go? It flows back to the heart.

Where does the heart send the pure, bright blood? To every part of the body. Where does it send the impure, dark blood? To the lungs. What are the lungs for? They give fresh air to the blood, and take impurities from it.

Did you ever see a physician place his ear over the chest to find out whether the lungs were healthy or not? He is able to tell this, because when the air passes into and out of the lungs, it makes peculiar sounds.

Do you think the lungs work all the time? You know we never stop breathing, not even at night. Yet, by watching your breathing, you will notice that there is a little time of rest between two breaths.

But the lungs work hard, and we should give them plenty of room and a good supply of fresh air.

ALCOHOL AND THE LUNGS.

We said, you remember, that the constant use of alcoholic liquors is likely to make the eyes, the nose, and the cheeks very red. The lungs are no exception to this; for strong drink causes too much blood to flow in their small blood vessels. This makes the person very liable to coughs and colds. In fact, all forms of lung trouble are more severe in those who use alcohol.

Persons who have been chilled by bathing, or in some other way, often take some alcoholic liquor. They say they do this "to prevent taking cold." This is a mistake; for the effect of alcohol is to lower the temperature of the body. Let us give you a far better way. When chilled from bathing, rub the surface of the body thoroughly with a towel, until the skin is warm and red. If chilled in some other way, drink a cup of hot water, or hot ginger tea.

TOBACCO AND THE LUNGS.

Do you think it is any wonder that hot tobacco smoke injures the throat and lungs? Smokers often have a dry, hacking cough, while the "smoker's sore throat" is very common. There is no cure for these troubles unless the use of tobacco be given up altogether. Inhaling the smoke, or drawing it into the lungs, is very injurious. How can one escape all these dangers? By refusing to begin the use of tobacco.

QUESTIONS.

1. Where does the heart send the dark blood?
2. How is the blood changed in the lungs?
3. How many lungs are there?
4. To what do we compare the inside of a lung?
5. Tell about the little air sacs.
6. Tell how they change in breathing.
7. What is said about the blood vessels in the lungs?
8. What changes the dark blood to a bright red?
9. Answer the questions asked on page 57.
10. How do alcoholic liquors affect the lungs?
11. Does tobacco injure the throat and lungs?

CHAPTER X.

FRESH AIR.

Can you give a good reason why we should have plenty of fresh air about us all the time? Because the air we breathe out contains many impurities, and certainly we do not wish to take these back into the body.

Can you expect the lungs to do their work well without plenty of room? Nature has given them all the room they need, but some persons wear their clothes so tight around the waist, that they make the lower part of the chest very small. Such persons cannot take a long, deep breath. How can you expect the body to grow and develop, if it be bound tightly in this way? Tight lacing crowds many organs out of place, and sooner or later injures the health. Give the lungs plenty of room.

How can you tell when the air about you is impure? It is not always possible to do so; but it is likely to be impure if it has a disagreeable odor, or if it has been closed in a room for some time, or if many persons have been in the room.

The pure, fresh, out-door air is what we need; it is the air in our houses and public buildings that is likely to be impure. It is not healthy to stay in a room and breathe the same air over and over again. The air can be easily changed by raising the lower sash of one window and lowering the upper sash of another. In large buildings there is usually some special arrangement for changing the air.

Some people seem to think that it is only necessary to have fresh air in the daytime, and they pay no attention to their sleeping rooms. But breathing goes on at night just as well as during the day. Therefore, our sleeping rooms should have a constant supply of fresh air. Never sleep in a tightly closed room.

During the winter there should be an open grate, or a ventilator, or some way of changing the air. During the warm nights of summer the windows can be opened wide; and even during the cold nights of winter it is safe to have the windows open an inch or two.

During the day, open the windows of your sleeping rooms and let in the fresh out-door air. There is nothing better than fresh air to make one sleep well.

Did you ever know a boy or a girl who could run very hard in playtime, and yet get very dull and sleepy in the schoolroom? The school is not a good place in which to sleep or to have the headache. What is the matter with our dull scholar? Well, sometimes pupils become dull because the air in the schoolroom is not good. Let in plenty of the pure air; there is nothing equal to it for making one love to study.

While so much has been said about breathing pure, out-door air, yet it may be overdone. We must learn to be careful in this as in all other things. We should avoid currents of air. If a current of air — a draught, as it is called — should strike you on the back of the neck, it might cause a severe cold. If you have been playing hard and the body is moist, you should be especially careful to avoid all currents of air.

Some persons are very careful to have pure air in every room of their houses, and yet they will often make it very impure by smoking cigars. We know a number of persons who are made quite ill by inhaling a small quantity of tobacco smoke; yet sometimes, as we walk along the streets, it is impossible to escape breathing the air thus poisoned.

QUESTIONS.

1. Why should we have plenty of fresh air about us?
2. What can you say about the room which the lungs need?
3. Where is the air likely to be impure?
4. How can we change the air in our houses?
5. What is said about the air in our sleeping rooms?
6. Give some ways of changing it.
7. What is said about currents of air?
8. How is pure air sometimes made impure?

CHAPTER XI.

ALCOHOL.

THE writer remembers very well how, when a boy, he used to watch for the first ripe apples, and, later in the year, how he waited for the ripening of the grapes. How he loved to eat those pleasant and harmless fruits! It seems too bad that the juices of such sweet fruits can be so changed as to cause great injury to many people. Yet we know that from these fruits such strong drinks as wine and brandy are made.

Is there anything in these fresh fruits that makes them so powerful to do harm? No, indeed; but when the juice is pressed out, it soon ceases to be sweet. What becomes of the sugar that made these fruits so sweet and pleasant? Let us tell you.

If you should press the juice from some ripe sweet apples, what would you have? You would have apple juice, which is simply a mixture of water and sugar, and a little apple flavor. This is called cider. Now suppose you take this cider and expose it to the warm air for a few hours, then go and look at it. What will you see? Small bubbles coming to the top.

When these bubbles appear, you say the cider is working, or fermenting. Is the cider still sweet to the taste? Not so sweet as it was at first; the sugar is beginning to disappear. "How can it disappear," do you ask? It is being changed into a gas and alcohol. The gas escapes in the form of the bubbles which you see; but the alcohol remains in the cider.

So we learn that alcohol is made from the sugar which is in the apples; in the same way alcohol is made from the sugar in grapes and other fruits.

Now, alcohol is a poison; and it is the alcohol in all the strong drinks which makes them so injurious. Any drink containing alcohol is dangerous, and should not be used. Alcohol may not kill at once those

who use only a little at a time; yet it is a
poison that greatly injures the health, causes
many diseases, and shortens life. It is also
true that some persons have been killed at
once by taking it in large doses.

But you want to know what makes the
sugar that is in the ripe fruits change
into gas and alcohol. Have you ever been
in a darkened room and looked at a ray of
sunlight as it entered? If so, you saw fine
particles of dust dancing in the light.
These seemed very small, did they not?
Yet there are still smaller particles of matter floating everywhere in the air, smaller
than we can see with the unaided eye.

Some of these tiny particles are called
ferments. Some of these ferments fall from
the air upon the stems and skins of the
fruit. When the juice of the fruits is
pressed out these ferments are washed into
it. Do you think, just because they are so
small they can do nothing? If so, you
are mistaken. They can change sugar into
alcohol. You can see when the ferments

are at work changing the sugar, by the bubbles that come to the surface.

The ferments are very numerous, and of many different kinds. They float about in the air, not only lighting on the skins and stems of the fruits, but falling into mixtures which may be exposed to the air. "Then," you ask, "if we could only keep these little ferments away from the sweet mixtures, the sugar would not change to alcohol, would it?" No; the sugar would remain in its natural condition.

The ferments that are washed into the juice when it is pressed out may be killed by boiling. Then, if the juice be bottled up so tightly that no more ferments can fall into it from the air, the sugar will not be changed. Now you understand why canning fruit will keep it sweet and good. No ferments can pass through the tightly sealed cans or jars to the sweet juices within.

You all know that dry sugar does not change in this way. Why is this? Because the sugar must first be dissolved, to make a sweet liquid in which the ferments can work.

Some boy says, " I thought beer was made from barley, and whiskey from corn. Certainly there is no sugar in these dry grains!" No, there is no sugar in them, but there is something from which sugar is made. Let us explain this, and you will see how it is brought about.

Did you ever break open a kernel of corn or cut into a grain of barley? Bring a kernel of corn with you to school and show your schoolmates how beautiful and white is the inside. This is the corn starch, with which you are all so familiar.

How can this starch ever become alcohol? Well, in the first place, it must be changed into sugar; and we know already how sugar, when dissolved in water, is changed into alcohol.

Do you know what would happen to the corn and barley if you should moisten them and keep them in a warm place? Certainly, every boy and girl knows the kernels would soon sprout and begin to grow. Now, as they sprout and grow, the starch changes to sugar. So here we are at last, with sugar from our corn and barley. But how do we get the sugar from these growing grains?

This is the way it is done : The brewer takes the corn and barley, and 'adds water to them until they begin to grow, then he knows that their starch is changed into sugar. He then grinds the grains or breaks them to pieces, and adds water to the ground mass. Soon the water dissolves out the sugar, and thus at last there is a sweet liquid. Then the brewer adds some yeast, which is a kind of ferment. The yeast changes the sugar of the sweet liquid into gas and alcohol.

Why do not the ferments change sugar into alcohol while it is in the ripe fruits? Because the skins of the apples and other fruits will not allow the ferments to reach the sweet juices within them.

CHAPTER XII.

THE ALCOHOLIC LIQUORS.

How many of you have ever eaten apples? Did you think it wrong to swallow the juice of the apples? Most certainly not. Yet you know cider is made from the juice of apples, and we shall tell you that cider is a harmful drink.

What, then, is the difference between the juice that is pressed from the apple at the mill, and that which you press from the apple by your own teeth? The difference is that there is no alcohol in the juice you get when you eat the apple, but there may be alcohol in the juice that comes from the mill.

After apple juice has been pressed out and left exposed to the warm air for a few hours, it begins to ferment. When the bubbles begin to rise and the froth gathers, we know that alcohol is being formed.

As soon as cider contains alcohol it is no longer a harmless drink. Alcohol usually begins to form in sweet cider within about six hours after the cider is made. As the ferments, day after day, change more of the sugar to alcohol, the cider is said to be growing "hard."

The person who begins to drink from a barrel of cider when it first comes from the press, and continues to drink daily the same amount, takes each day more and more alcohol.

Why will this do him harm? Because, for one reason, the alcohol in the cider may make him like alcohol so well that he will care more for it than for anything else. Even a little alcohol has the power to create an appetite for more.

For this reason it is never safe to use drinks that contain even a small amount of alcohol. Many a person who did not know this has gained a craving for strong alcoholic liquors simply by drinking cider.

Do you remember how beer is made from

barley? Ale and porter are made in much the same way.

Why should we not drink beer? Because it has the power to do great harm.

Beer has power to dull the mind and make one less able to think quickly and clearly.

Beer has power to create the craving that calls for the stronger alcoholic liquors.

How do we know that beer has the power to do all these things? Because it has done them again and again. What it has done it has power to do again.

Some people wisely think that brewer's beer is very injurious. So they make a kind of their own from roots and hops. They add water to these and apply heat to get the strength from them. Then they add some sugar and yeast.

Do you think this homemade beer is harmless? Watch the mixture a few days, and you can tell. Notice the bubbles of gas rising to the surface, showing that the sugar is changing into gas and alcohol.

The gas escapes, but the alcohol remains to form a part of the root beer or hop beer. Now you know the mixture is harmful; for it contains alcohol.

Do you know of any fruit that looks prettier than a bunch of grapes? Grapes are not only beautiful, but they are also pleasant to the taste. The juice you get when you eat grapes is sweet and healthful; ferments cannot change its sugar to alcohol when it is in the grapes. But when this juice is pressed out, the ferments that are washed into it quickly begin to change its sugar into alcohol.

The alcohol that the ferments form in the liquid remains in it, and makes it poisonous. Thus we see why wine is a harmful drink, though made from healthful grapes.

The alcohol in wine, like that in beer and cider, has the power to create an appetite for more. Therefore the only safe rule with wine is never to drink it at all.

Some persons will not drink wine that is

bought at a store, so they make it themselves. They take the juice of the grape, currant, or elderberry and allow it to ferment, and then bottle it up for home use. But these homemade wines often contain more alcohol than the others, and are therefore more harmful.

Whiskey, brandy, and rum are very powerful drinks. They are at least one half pure alcohol, and sometimes they are even stronger. Brandy is usually made from wine and cider; whiskey from corn, barley, and other grains; and rum from molasses.

We hear a great deal said about liquors being pure. Many people say that if only the best of grains and fruits were used, and if no drugs of any kind were added, then the liquors would be pure and wholesome. What a great mistake is this!

It is true that some liquors are made more harmful by having mixed with them many poisonous drugs; but any liquor that contains alcohol is both dangerous and harmful. It is the presence of this poison that makes all alcoholic liquors so highly injurious.

———•———

"Apples, ripe apples, we'll pick from the trees,
  But cider — no cider for us, if you please.
  Grapes, purple grapes, for your eating and mine,
  But we'll turn down our glasses where pours
      the red wine.

"Barley, fresh barley, we'll welcome as bread,
  But when made into beer it is poison instead.
  We'll enjoy all the good things God maketh to
      grow,
  When men change them to poisons, we'll
      bravely say, 'No.'"

QUESTIONS.

1. When is apple juice harmful?
2. How may we know when alcohol is being formed?
3. What is the harm in drinking hard cider?
4. Give some reasons why we should not drink beer.
5. What shows us that homemade beer must be injurious?
6. What is a safe rule with wine?
7. Why is this the only safe rule?
8. What makes all alcoholic liquors so injurious?
9. Repeat together the two verses.

CHAPTER XIII.

THE EFFECTS OF ALCOHOL.

WHEN you come running into the house after a hearty play, very warm and thirsty, a glass of cool water quenches your thirst, does it not? It certainly does not make you more thirsty, so that you desire more and more of the water! Indeed, when you come running into the house the next day, as warm and thirsty as before, the same amount of water will quench your thirst.

Drinks containing alcohol differ from water in this respect; instead of quenching thirst they create a thirst. The person who uses strong drink is likely to be satisfied with a small amount for a short time only.

The first glass of beer has the power to create a desire for another, until one glass is not sufficient; later on, beer does not satisfy, and the stronger drinks are craved. In this way the appetite for strong drink is often formed. When this appetite is well fixed, it sometimes completely masters the person.

The life of a drinking man is often divided into two chapters. The same words are in each chapter; but, alas! how different is their meaning!—Chapter I., The man could stop drinking if he would; Chapter II., The man would stop drinking if he could.

Is not such a power terrible? Yes, indeed; it is one of the most fearful things that can be said against alcohol.

Some of the very strongest and wisest men have thought that they need not fear; for this appetite could never affect them. But too often they have discovered that it has completely conquered them. Students who have always mastered the hardest lessons have been completely mastered themselves by this power. Soldiers who have never yielded to the enemy in battle have found that they had to yield to the power of strong drink.

Would you like to know how to escape from this terrible power? Do you wish that it may never affect you in any way? Then refuse to take the first glass of cider, beer, wine, or any drink that contains alcohol.

Did you ever hear a boy say that he knows this power can never affect him? Perhaps he thinks that if he should begin the use of strong drink, he could stop it at any time when he so desires. But, my boy, that is not what the study of alcohol teaches. We should all remember that a little alcohol has the power to create an uncontrollable appetite for more. None are sure of escape, if they begin its use. There is but one safe course to pursue: *Refuse to take the first glass.*

Shall we give you another reason why it is dangerous to take even a single glass? Because a young person may not know that he has any desire for strong drink, until he has tasted some of the lighter drinks, or some sauce flavored with wine. It is easy to begin, "little by little," to walk in the road that leads to ruin and despair. It is also easy to begin in another road that leads to success and happiness.

———•———

"'Little by little,' said a thoughtful boy,
'Moment by moment I'll well employ,
Learning a little every day,
And not spend all my time in play;
And still this rule in my mind shall dwell,—
Whatever I do, I'll do it well.
Little by little, I'll learn to know
The treasured wisdom of long ago.
And one of these days perhaps we'll see
That the world will be the better for me.'

 . . . . . .

And do you not think that this simple plan
Will make him a wiser and better man?"

QUESTIONS.

1. How do drinks containing alcohol differ from water?
2. Why is it harmful to drink beer?
3. What is said of the power of strong drink?
4. Who have been overcome by this power?
5. What is the only safe rule?

CHAPTER XIV.

TOBACCO.

DID you ever see more frightful-looking objects than the signs in front of many tobacco shops? Each time you look at these hideous figures of Indians, you should be reminded that the habit of using tobacco came to us from the savages.

FIG. 15. The tobacco plant.

Probably you all know that tobacco is made from the leaves of a plant. But do you know why it is that the tobacco leaf is used instead of the leaf of the beet or the cabbage? It is because there is in tobacco a substance called nicotine, not found in the others. This is a powerful poison, a single drop of it being sufficient to kill an animal the size of a dog.

Perhaps you have heard some of the older boys tell how sick the first use of tobacco made them. It was because they were suffering from the poisonous effects of the nicotine. If these boys tell you that the headache and the vomiting soon disappear, perhaps they do not tell you about the slower effects of this poison.

Can you name a single animal that will have anything to do with tobacco? None of the lower animals with which we are familiar ever touch it; nearly all insects keep away from it; and plants, when placed in a room where there is a strong odor of it, wither and die.

Did you ever ask persons who use tobacco if it harms them? If so, perhaps some of them have told you that they are sure it does not; while others say they know it harms them, but they cannot break away from the habit. It is certainly true that tobacco injures those who use it, — some more than others. Even those who think they are not harmed by its use, would find themselves much better off without it.

The reason why so many grown persons do not appear to suffer from using tobacco, is probably because they did not begin its use until their bodies had attained full growth.

It is a positive fact that tobacco is very harmful to the young. We do not believe there is a single exception to this rule. Tobacco does immense harm to those who use it while the body is growing and developing. Its effects are not only serious, but they are lasting. Here is a rule which you should all remember : *The younger the person using tobacco, the more serious will be its effects.*

Did you know that twenty-nine States have passed laws forbidding the sale of tobacco to young persons? Even the United States Government will not allow the boys whom it is training to be soldiers or sailors to use tobacco in any form. Now can you tell why such laws are passed? Because the men who make the laws see that the use of tobacco is seriously injuring the boys of our country.

Do you think we are talking all this time about cigars only? No, indeed. We have our minds on the little cigarettes, too. Boys sometimes think because cigarettes are so small, and do not contain strong tobacco, there cannot be much harm in using them. Such boys make a great mistake. Cigarettes injure every boy who uses them. It is equally true that many boys have their health broken, their minds injured, their good name destroyed,

Fig. 16. The poppy, or opium plant.

and all their bright prospects for life ruined by these same little cigarettes.

Did you know that sometimes the poorest tobacco which can be procured, is used in making cigarettes, and that it is often mixed with opium? Shall we tell you what makes the cigarette paper so very white?

Because it is often bleached with a mixture containing arsenic. So taking it altogether, the cigarette is poisonous, and is a dangerous thing to use.

Suppose you ask one of your playmates, "Why do you eat your dinner?" he will probably answer, "Because I am hungry." Ask him, "Why do you drink a glass of water?" he will tell you, "Because I am thirsty." He is always ready to give you a reasonable answer to such questions, is he not? But do you think any boy could give you a good reason for smoking?

Let any boy who smokes tell one good reason, if he can, why he uses cigarettes. There is no reason why boys should smoke, and many reasons why they should not.

———•———

"Cigarettes, they say, are harmless, —
  Just a tiny little roll!
But the appetite they waken
  Soon might get beyond control;
And tobacco chains would bind us,
  Slaves in body and in soul."

CHAPTER XV.

REASONS WHY BOYS SHOULD NOT SMOKE.

ONE of the first things we notice about a boy who smokes is that when meal time comes he is not hungry. He does not eat enough good food, and without plenty of food his body cannot grow and become strong. *Tobacco takes away the appetite.*

Such a boy often complains of being dizzy. He says he has a rush of blood to the head. He is troubled with horrible dreams, and awakes in the morning with a dull, heavy headache. He goes to school, but because he cannot study well, his standing in his classes is low. *Tobacco affects the brain.*

Notice the want of neatness in the boy who smokes! His teeth are dark colored; they have an offensive appearance; and the odor of the tobacco clings to his clothes. *Smoking is a filthy habit.*

Do boys run away from home to eat their supper? Do they hide to comb their hair? Yet they will go away from home and hide to smoke their cigarettes. Why is this? Because they know that the practice is not a good one, and they are ashamed of it. Boys will deny that they use tobacco, when they will not tell a falsehood about anything else for the whole world. Boys, do you wish to begin a practice like this, — one which is so unmanly that many who are engaged in it will deny it? *Smoking makes boys deceitful.*

One of the sad things we have noticed as a result of smoking cigarettes, is that the boys who smoke are very likely to drink when they get older. The use of tobacco very early in life often creates a desire for strong drink. *Smoking often leads to drinking.*

Count how many sentences there are in this chapter printed in Italics. Five, are there not? Read them over again. Do you not think each sentence gives a good reason why boys should never smoke? Are not these enough to show that you are much better off without tobacco?

But suppose the boy who smokes wishes to defend himself. What will he say? Let him begin to read all the books on physiology, study all there is said about the care of the health; and then tell us if he has found a single good thing about the use of tobacco. The best students and writers agree that tobacco is harmful.

Learn to say, "NO!"

———•———

"Say *no!* to tobacco, that poisonous weed;
  Say *no!* to all evils; they only can lead
  To shame and to sorrow. Oh, shun them, my
    boy,
  For wisdom's fair pathway of peace and of
    joy."

CHAPTER XVI.

THE MUSCLES.

DID you ever see a piece of beefsteak before it was cooked? "Oh, yes, many times," you answer. "It is soft, and of a deep red color." Can you tell the name of the lean meat which makes the flesh of animals? It is called muscle.

How many muscles are there in the body? There are as many as five hundred, each one having a name and some special work to do. Are they all of the same size? No, for some are very large and long, reaching from the hip to the knee; while others are so small that they can scarcely be seen with the unaided eye. Do these muscles form a large or a small part of the body? We will let you decide this after we tell you that nearly one half the weight of the body is due to the muscles.

Can you tell what the muscles are for? Well, the cheeks and the lips are nearly all muscle; and what is one of their uses? They enclose the mouth. Therefore, some of the muscles make walls for cavities.

But the muscles have a more important use. What is it? They move the different parts of the body. Did you ever notice under what complete control you have your muscles? You can use one of them only, as in bending the end of a finger, or you can use a very large number of them, as in walking or running.

Why is it the muscles are of such great use to us? Simply because they can shorten and then lengthen again. Now place your left hand over the front of your right arm and raise your forearm. "Oh," you say, "this is trying my muscle." Yes, and do you notice that the muscle swells and becomes harder? When it does this, it shortens. We say it contracts. How do we know the muscle shortens? Because it moves the part to which it is fastened.

Can we make all the muscles contract whenever we wish? Let us experiment a little and so find out. We certainly can

move the hands, the arms, the head, and many parts of the face, as often as we like. But how is it with the heart? The heart is made of muscle, yet it continues to beat, even during sleep, and we have no power to change its action. From this we learn that there are a few muscles we cannot control.

Fig. 17. The upper part of the figure shows the muscles, while the lower part shows the slender, white tendons at the wrist.

Some of the muscles are fastened directly to the bones; while others end in white shining cords which are attached to the bones. These cords are called tendons. Did you ever notice them on the back of your hand? Bend your fingers back and forth; perhaps you will be able to see them. Now the muscles

which move your fingers are in the forearm; but when they are near the wrist,
they end in these tendons, as shown in
Fig. 17.

Why is it your fingers move, when the
muscles moving them are in the forearm?
Because when the muscles contract, they
pull on these cords or tendons, which are
fastened to the fingers.

With thick muscles around the fingers to
move them, think what a large and clumsy
hand you would have! Do you not see
how the tendons save room, allow the parts
to move more easily, and aid in giving a
much better shape to the body?

Now let us look at Figs. 18 and 19, and
see if we can learn how the muscles move
parts of the body. Look at Fig. 18 first.
Imagine that the muscle on the front of
the arm contracts, or shortens, pulling on
the cord, or tendon, which is fastened to the
bone of the forearm. As this muscle shortens, it would raise the forearm and the hand
with it, would it not?

By looking at the next figure, it is easy
to see that if the muscle in front shortens,
it will raise the toes; while if the muscle
at the back shortens, the heel will be raised
and the toes lowered. Can you tell now

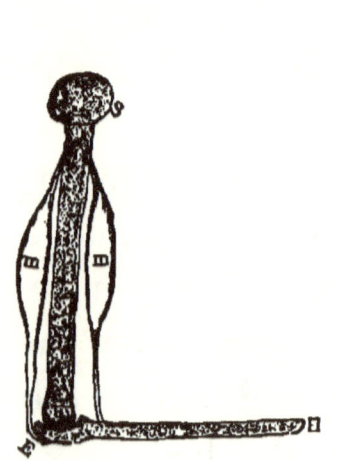

Fig. 18. S, the shoulder; E, the elbow;
H, the hand; M, the muscles.

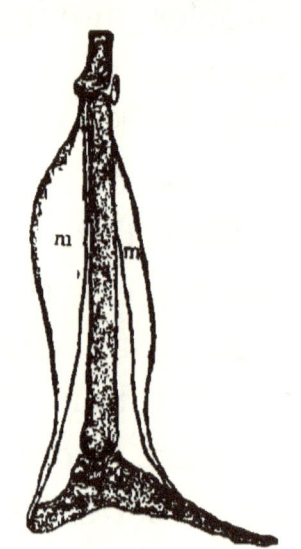

Fig. 19. Muscles of the leg.

what causes all the movements of the
body? Certainly; the contraction of the
muscles.

The contraction of certain muscles lifts
the brow and makes a smile pass over the
face; while the contraction of other muscles
causes a frown or look of displeasure.

"Go and stand before the glass
   And some ugly thought contrive,
And my word will come to pass
   Just as sure as you're alive.

"What you have and what you lack,
   All the same as what you wear,
You will see reflected back;
   So, my little folks, take care!

"And not only in the glass
   Will your secrets come to view;
All beholders, as they pass,
   Will perceive and know them too.

"Cherish what is good, and drive
   Evil thoughts and feelings far;
For as sure as you're alive,
   You will show for what you are."

QUESTIONS.

1. Are there many muscles in the body?
2. Give one use of the muscles.
3. Give a more important use.
4. Why is it the muscles are of such great use to us?
5. Can we control all the muscles in the body?
6. Tell something about the tendons.
7. How is the forearm raised?

CHAPTER XVII.

EXERCISE.

ARE all the boys and girls in your school of equal strength? Cannot some of them run faster than others? Now what is the reason of this? Your muscles are all alike. Of course sickness and poor health will keep some of you weak; but why is it that some boys always seem to be so much stronger than others, who are in the same good health? Well, one reason of this is because the stronger boy has given his muscles more work to do.

If we wish to keep our muscles healthy and strong, they must be made to work. How many of you have ever seen a blacksmith? Notice how large are his arms! What a hard blow he can strike! Do you think his arms were always so large and strong? No, indeed, it was the hard work he gave them to do which made them grow.

And he keeps them large and stout because he continues his hard work.

Do you know that you can make the muscles of your arm nearly all disappear? This can be done by keeping the arm in a sling for a number of weeks. For without exercise the muscles will become thin and soft, and nearly waste away.

But you must not think that the muscles are the only parts aided by exercise. How is it when you are taking a hard run? You breathe faster, and take in more fresh air. Your heart beats faster, and the blood flows more freely through your body. What is the result of all this? You have a good appetite; you sleep well; and the whole body is greatly benefited.

Do you think much of a boy who is all muscle and no brain? Or are you pleased to hear of a boy who is very learned and yet suffers pain all the time? No, indeed. We all prefer to see a healthy body and a strong mind in the same person. Do you think from what we have said that you can have both of these if you exercise the one and neglect the other? Certainly not. Therefore play heartily and study earnestly.

Do you think there is very much sport in walking? Yet it is one of the very best exercises for young and old. But let us combine pleasure with our exercise. So we will choose the ball in summer, and the sled and skates in winter. Of course running and jumping are always in season. But all this exercise will not do much good if taken in a close room. It is the fresh, pure air that is needed. No indoor exercise can possibly take the place of exercise in the open air.

We rarely hear of young boys studying too hard, yet they do sometimes play until the body is completely tired out. We often hear of girls who skip the rope until they are faint and ill. Now this is not the proper way to exercise. It must be remembered that too violent exercise may cause severe illness. Do you want to know why we tell you so much about the exercise of the muscles in the open air? Because it promotes good health, bringing with it a desire for the exercise of the mind in the schoolroom.

> "I must be active every hour,
> And do my Maker's will;
> If but a ray can paint the flower,
> A raindrop swell the rill,
> I know in me there is a power
> Some humble place to fill."

DOES ALCOHOL GIVE STRENGTH?

Can a man walk better if he takes strong drink? Can he do more hard work if he is under the influence of alcohol? These are very important questions. Many people have to work hard. If they could only do more work, they would be able to earn more money. Now do you think that alcohol gives strength to the muscles?

Notice a person who is under the influence of strong drink! He has a staggering gait; his tongue is thick; and his fingers are clumsy. Do you think the alcohol has made his muscles stronger? Instead of being stronger they are weaker, are they not? Only a little more strong drink and the muscles would not hold the body up; the body would fall and become perfectly helpless. We shall learn in a later chapter that the delicate nerves have much to do in bringing about this result.

But, you ask, "Suppose a person should take only a small amount of alcohol, as a glass or two of beer, or a glass of wine or whiskey, would not this give strength to his muscles?" No, indeed; for it is positively known that alcohol weakens the muscles. The workman with his ale or beer cannot do so much work as he can do without it.

> "Let us do the work we do
>   With a true and earnest zeal;
>   Bend our sinews to the task,
>   Put our shoulders to the wheel.
>
> "Though our duty may be hard,
>   Look not on it as an ill;
>   If it be an honest task,
>   Do it with an honest will."

CHAPTER XVIII.

THE CLOTHING.

Do you know why your body is chilly
and cold when exposed to the air? It is
because the air about you is generally colder
than the body; so the body gives out its
heat to the air. Is it possible to put something around the body to keep the heat in?
Why, yes, that is easily done; put on some
clothing. But does the clothing make the
heat? No, the body itself does that; the
clothing simply keeps the heat from leaving
the body.

The clothing also protects the body from
the direct rays of the sun; from the storms
of rain and snow; and from many injuries.
It is also an ornament to the body.

Now that you know the uses of clothing, would you advise any one to wear as
heavy clothing in summer as in winter?
No, indeed, even the animals teach us better

than this. In the spring they shed their coats of long hair, so that during the summer their clothing may be lighter and thinner. Yet some people make a great mistake in laying aside the flannels of winter too early. Better wait until the summer weather is surely at hand before running any risk of taking cold.

How many of you have had a sore throat, or a cold? We presume nearly every one has suffered in this way. Do you wish to be your own doctor, and cure yourself of a cold? This, then, is a very good way: If your throat is a little sore and you feel that you have taken cold, try a hot foot-bath; drink a bowlful of hot ginger tea, or if you would prefer it, hot lemonade; undress and go to bed; cover up well; and thus cause the perspiration to flow freely. In this way you can many times break up a cold at its beginning, and perhaps prevent a long sickness. You must be very careful, however, not to allow the body to cool too quickly after such treatment.

All the clothing should be changed at night. Never sleep in any garment that has been worn during the day. If caught in a storm, hasten home, and change the damp clothing for dry. Do not go about with damp feet. A great many sore throats and colds have been caused by wet feet.

Do you think that clothing must be very expensive in order to look attractive? We do not. We have seen boys and girls dressed in a most expensive manner, and yet there was something about their clothing that was not pleasing. Remember, the simplest garments look well, if they are neat and clean.

> THE PERSON IS OF MORE VALUE THAN HIS COAT.

DOES ALCOHOL WARM THE BODY?

Did you ever take a long drive in the cold? How did you manage to keep warm? You put on extra clothing, did you not? Perhaps you had something warm to place at your feet. Did you take a good, warm meal just before you started? Then so much the better.

Yet some persons think that they know a better way than this. They say that before starting on a cold journey they always take a glass of wine, "for wine warms the body and keeps one from taking cold." Is there any truth in this? Does wine or brandy or any strong drink warm the whole body? No, indeed. Yet these persons say it does. Now, why is it that they are so mistaken? Because the alcohol makes more blood go to the skin. This makes the skin feel warmer; so the person thinks his whole body is warmer.

But the skin is warmer for only a few moments. When the blood is in the skin it is near the cool air, and thus is soon cooled. When this blood leaves the skin, it passes through the other parts of the body, cooling them on its way. Is this clear to you? Perhaps some questions and answers will make it more clear.

Does a full dose of wine or brandy make the skin warmer? Yes.

Why? Because it sends more blood to the skin.

Does this last long? Only for a very short time.

Are the deeper parts of the body warmed? No, only the skin.

Then is the whole body warmed by strong drink? No.

Is it often made colder? Yes, alcoholic liquors lower the warmth of the body.

Would you advise taking wine, or any other alcoholic drink, on a cold day? No, indeed. It would only make the body still colder.

If alcohol could make the body warm, then those persons who have traveled in very cold countries would use it a great deal, would they not? Yet all the great Arctic explorers tell us that they never allowed the use of a single drop of alcoholic liquors. They all say that they could not have endured the extreme cold if they **had** used liquors.

Persons who have traveled in the hottest countries, and officers who have charge of the soldiers in such places, write that they endure the excessive heat very much better without a drop of any strong drink.

Thus we learn that strong drink is not good for men living in cold countries, nor for those in very warm countries. It will not feed us, neither will it clothe us. It seems to bring no good to any one, and may cause great harm to every one who uses it. Then what do you think we would better do with it? Leave it entirely alone.

> " Honor and virtue, love and truth,
> All the glory and pride of youth,
> Hope of manhood, the wreath of fame,
> High endeavor and noble aim, —
> These are the treasures thrown away
> As the price of a drink from day to day."

QUESTIONS.

1. How does clothing add to the comfort of the body?
2. What is said about damp clothing and wet feet?
3. Why do not Arctic travelers use alcoholic drinks?
4. What should we do with alcoholic liquors?

CHAPTER XIX.

THE SKIN.

CAN you tell of a garment given us by Nature that fits the body nicely and yet never wears out? Yes, indeed; it is the skin. Have you ever noticed how soft and tight-fitting it is? Think how much wear there must be on this garment. It is constantly rubbing against the clothing, while every use of the towel in bathing must wear upon it greatly. Yet it never wears out. The blood is always bringing it food, keeping it in perfect repair.

You know that sometimes you can prick yourself with a pin and yet not cause a flow of blood; while if the pin should go into the skin a little deeper, blood would surely flow. How do you account for this? Because the outer part of the skin has no blood vessels. How fortunate is this! If the blood vessels came to the very outside of the skin, every little bruise or scratch would cause the flow of blood.

A slight scratch of the pin does not hurt very much, does it? This is because there are no nerves in the outer part. How fortunate again! For if the nerves came to the surface also, everything we touched would give us severe pain.

You do not think there are many interesting things found deep in the skin, do you? Yet we have already mentioned two, the blood vessels and the nerves. But these are found everywhere. You wish to know of something found in the skin that we do not find elsewhere, do you? Well, we will mention three things for you to remember: the hair, the sweat glands, and the oil glands.

Have you ever noticed what smooth and glossy hair some persons have? Yet they may never use any kind of hair oil. Let us see if we can explain this. Deep in the skin there are some glands which make

an oily substance that is poured around
the base of each
hair. If the scalp
is healthy, the oil
glands will fur-
nish enough oil
to keep the hair
soft and smooth.
If you look at
Fig. 20, you will
see that part of
a hair which is
within its sheath,
beneath the skin.
Large oil glands
are seen on either
side of it.

Sometimes dur-
ing the warm
weather of sum-
mer, or after you
have been work-
ing or playing
hard, the whole

Fig. 20. A human hair (H), as it appears
beneath the skin, in its sheath. G, the oil
gland, which pours an oily substance around
the hair.

body becomes covered with moisture. Often the moisture gathers in little drops of water on the face. This moisture is called perspiration. Where do you suppose it comes

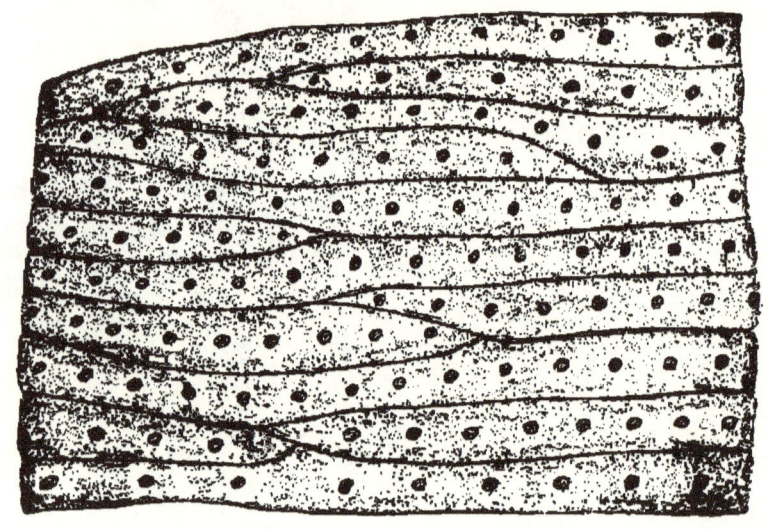

FIG. 21.   The surface of the skin as seen with a magnifying glass.

from?   It comes from glands called the sweat glands.

Look carefully at the palm of your hand, or the inside of your fingers, and notice some minute lines or ridges. Now if you could look at these with a magnifying glass, they would appear like Fig. 21.   Do you notice in the figure some little round pits? You could see these pits nicely on your own hand, if you had a magnifying glass. Now, the little pits are the openings of the sweat glands. These openings are sometimes called the pores of the skin. If you look at Fig. 22, you will see some of these sweat glands, looking like coiled tubes, down in the skin. The perspiration passes up the long, narrow tubes to the surface of the skin.

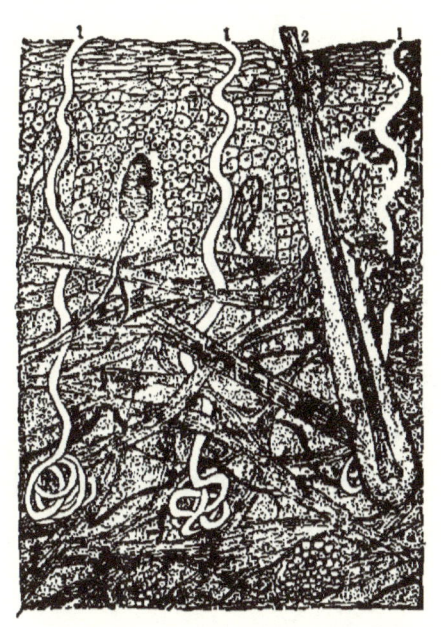

Fig. 22. (1) The narrow tubes which bring the perspiration to the surface from the sweat glands below. The sweat glands appear like closely coiled tubes. (2) A hair. (This is the same as Fig. 20.)

From each little pore there comes only a small part of a drop of perspiration; yet, taken together, they make enough moisture to be seen. Sometimes the moisture gathers in great drops on the forehead and face.

Do you know that this perspiration is coming through the skin all the time, even during the coldest weather of winter? Yet this is true. You did not know it, because there is not always enough of the perspiration to make it seen or felt. Do you think the perspiration is pure water? No; it is not. There are dissolved in it salts and impurities which must be removed from the body. When the perspiration dries on the body, what becomes of the salts and impurities? They remain on the skin. Do you think these should remain there, closing up the minute pores? Certainly not; they should be removed daily by the bath.

Be careful not to let the body cool too quickly when you are perspiring freely. After any hearty exercise, let the body cool gradually. Throw some light clothing over the shoulders, and avoid currents of air. Be cautious also about drinking too much cold water. Iced water at such times is especially bad.

How many of our girls keep a bird? You think that the bird must have a bath every morning, do you not? Now do you think that birds are more important than boys and girls? Our bodies certainly need bathing much more frequently than do the birds' bodies. The whole body should be bathed at least once each day.

When is the best time to bathe? When does your bird have his bath? In the morning? And the morning is the best time for you. A bath at bedtime is refreshing and will often cause a better night's rest. But a cool bath in the morning, immediately after rising, is the best. By bathing each day, it is only necessary to have a basin of water, a sponge or wash cloth, and a towel. Moisten a portion of the body at a time and wipe quickly. The morning bath makes one feel better all through the day. Once a week a thorough bath, with soap and warm water, should be taken.

CHAPTER XX.

THE BONES.

You have been learning about muscles, blood vessels, and the skin. If our bodies were made only of these soft parts, do you think they would keep their proper shape? Could we run and jump, if our limbs were only a mass of flesh? What do you suppose gives such a firm support to our bodies? Take hold of your arm and feel how hard it is in the center. We call these hard parts the support or framework of the body. We need not tell you that this framework is made of a large number of bones.

What are bones for? They give proper shape to the body; they give support to the soft flesh; and they also protect many delicate parts from injury. They have still another important use. Nearly all the muscles are fastened to them. You have already learned how the muscles move the bones, as in walking, running, and jumping.

Some of the bones are large and round, while others are thin and flat. How many bones do you suppose there are in the body? Over two hundred.

Bones look very solid to you, do they not? Yet if you should saw a fresh bone open, you would find that the center of it is not hard. It is filled with a soft substance called marrow. But you will not find this marrow in the old bones you might pick up in the fields.

Even the outer part of the bone, that looks so very solid to you, has minute

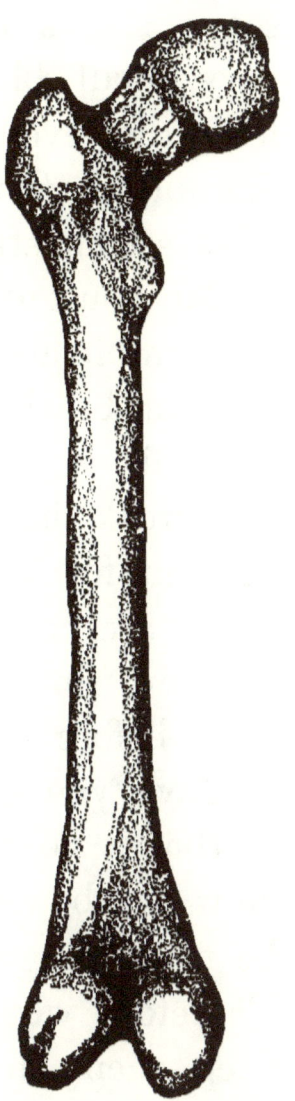

Fig. 23. The thigh bone, the largest bone in the body.

openings, or holes, in it. You cannot see these with the unaided eye, yet the microscope shows them. They are filled with very small blood vessels. From this we learn that even so hard a substance as bone has blood flowing through all its parts. This seems strange, does it not?

Can you tell why it is that boys and girls can tumble about and take such heavy falls without breaking their bones? During old age this is not so; sometimes a slight fall will break the largest bone. How can you account for this? Because early in life the bones are neither so hard nor so brittle as they are during old age. They will even bend before they break.

Have you ever seen a young tree bent, so that it is growing in an unnatural way? Now the bones, when they are young, can be made to grow in very unnatural shapes. Therefore we should be very careful to keep them in their natural positions by dressing, sitting, and walking in a proper manner.

CHAPTER XXI.

THE SKELETON AND THE JOINTS.

Can you think of a good name for the bony framework of the body? Let us call it the skeleton. That we may study it better, we will divide the skeleton into three parts,—the bones of the head, the bones of the trunk, and the bones of the limbs.

What are the bones of the head for? As you see, they make a pretty tight box. We will name this box the skull. Are there any holes in the skull? Yes, a few. They allow the nerves and the blood vessels to pass in and out. Why is the skull in the form of a tight box? In order that it may form a complete covering for the delicate brain. Think a moment, and then tell us of some other delicate parts which it protects. We can think of four; can you? Count them and see: There are the eyes, the ears, the nose, and the tongue.

Why do we call a certain part of the body the trunk? Well, why do you call a certain part of a tree by that name? You speak of the trunk of a tree, do you not? Yes, because the trunk is the main part of the tree. So the trunk is the main part of the body. At the back of the trunk is the back-bone; in front is the breast bone; on the sides are the ribs; and at the lower part are the hip bones.

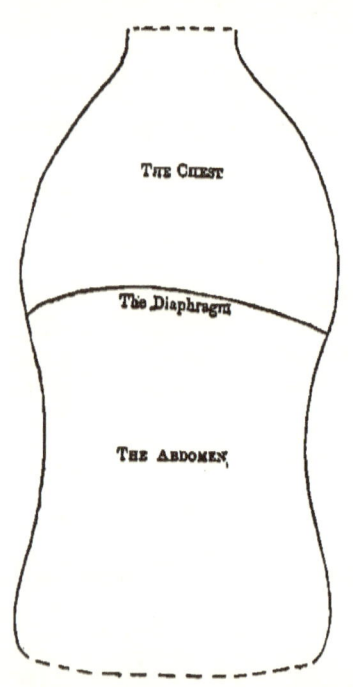

FIG. 24. The trunk, or the main part of the body.

Look at Fig. 24, and notice how the trunk is divided into two parts, by a thin arch of muscle. This arch is called by a very hard name, the diaphragm. It means a fence or wall. This arch is also shown at D, in Fig. 11, and at 6, in Fig. 13. So there are two large rooms in the trunk.

What shall we name the room above this arch? Let us call it the chest. What are those slender, curved bones forming the sides of the chest, and showing so clearly in Fig. 13? They are the ribs; and there are twelve of them on either side. You can easily feel the ribs, but it is not easy to count the whole number.

What is the name of the large room below the arch? It is called the abdomen. Are there any bony walls around this room? No, but the muscles and the skin make a firm, strong covering for the parts within. If you will look at Fig. 13 again, you will see what organs are in each of these rooms.

Run your hand across the front of the upper part of your chest. Do you feel two slender bones there? These are called the collar bones. One end of each collar bone is shown at 2, Fig. 13. Back of each collar bone, forming the back part of the shoulder, is a much larger bone, called the shoulder blade. How many bones do you think there are between the shoulder and the

elbow? Only one. The upper end fits into
the shoulder blade to make the shoulder
joint; and the lower end fits into another
bone to make
the elbow
joint.

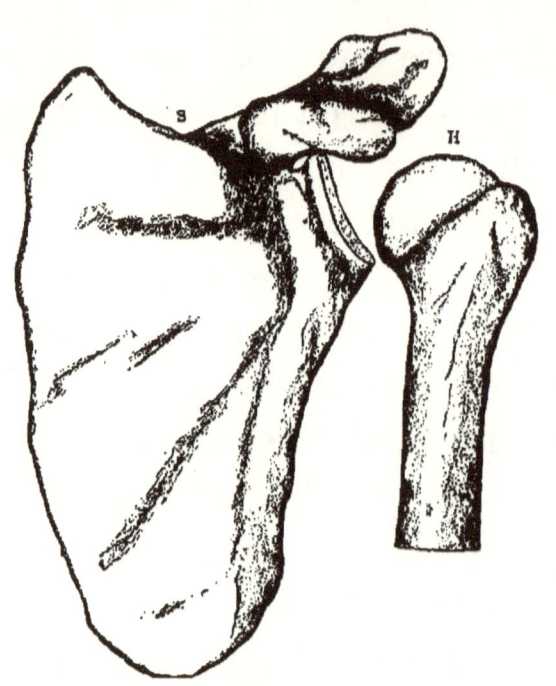

How many
bones can you
feel between
the elbow and
the wrist?
One or two?
There are two,
placed side by
side, and many
of you can feel
them, if you
try, near the

FIG. 25.   The shoulder joint. S, the shoulder
blade; H, the large bone of the arm.

wrist. A number of small bones make the
hand. Now count and see if you have five
large bones belonging to each upper ex-
tremity. The collar bone, the shoulder
blade, the large bone of the arm, and the
two bones placed side by side.

The bones of the lower limbs are much like those of the upper. The largest bone fits into the side of a hip bone to make the hip joint. This long bone extending from the hip to the knee is the largest bone in

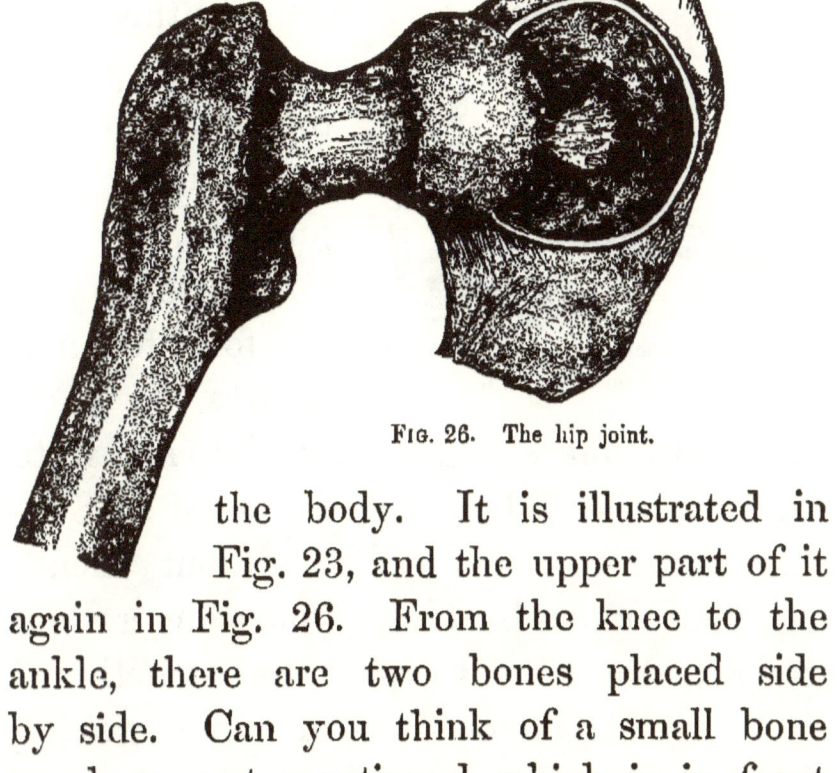

Fig. 26.   The hip joint.

the body. It is illustrated in Fig. 23, and the upper part of it again in Fig. 26. From the knee to the ankle, there are two bones placed side by side. Can you think of a small bone we have not mentioned which is in front of the knee joint? Oh, yes; the knee-pan.

Did you ever notice that not all of the bottom of the foot rests upon the floor? This is because the small bones in the foot are arranged in the form of an arch. What is this arch for? Notice the spring to a wagon; it is made in the form of an arch, is it not? So this arch in the foot acts as a spring, preventing the body from being jarred too severely, as in running and jumping.

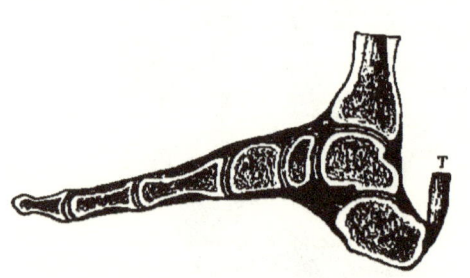

FIG. 27.   The bones of the foot arranged in the form of an arch.

Suppose you try, for a few moments, to keep your arm out straight, not allowing it to bend at the elbow in the least! Suppose you try to walk without bending your knees! Keep your fingers out straight, then try to pick up something! You would have a hard time getting along in this way, would you not? How fortunate it is that we have joints in our bodies!

Is it very hard work to move the joints of your fingers? No, indeed. They move easily and smoothly. How does the engineer keep the joints of his engine so that they always move easily and smoothly? He oils them, does he not? Now, do you know that all of your joints are kept moist with a fluid? It answers the same purpose as oil. This fluid is called the joint water.

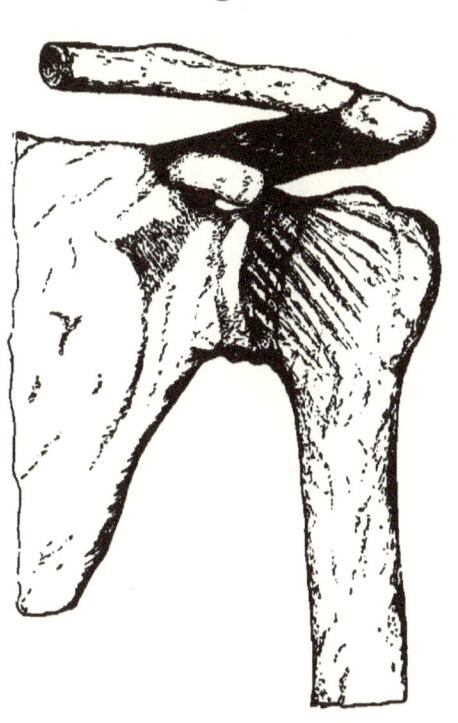

FIG. 28.   The shoulder joint, covered by its ligaments.

What holds the ends of the bones together at the joints? Some strong white bands of tissue called ligaments. Look at Fig. 28 and see how these bands completely cover the bones of the shoulder joint. Yet beneath the bands we know that the bones look as in Fig. 25.

Did you ever have a bone get "out of joint?" Was it very painful? How could it get out of place if these bands of tissue were around it? Why, the bone broke its way through the bands.

Did you ever "sprain" your ankle or your wrist? A sprain is sometimes very painful and causes trouble for a long time. The bones are not injured in a sprain. It is the ligaments that are injured.

QUESTIONS.

1. What is the name of the framework of the body?
2. Into how many parts do we divide the skeleton?
3. What is within the skull?
4. What other parts does the skull protect?
5. What is the name of the main part of the body?
6. What is at the back of the trunk? In front? On the sides?
7. What divides the trunk into two parts?
8. What name is given to the part above the diaphragm?
9. Where are the collar bones?
10. What bone is back of each collar bone?
11. How many bones between the shoulder and the elbow? Between the elbow and the wrist?
12. Which is the largest bone in the body?
13. Does all of the bottom of the foot rest upon the floor? Why not?
14. What keeps the joints moist?
15. What are ligaments for?
16. What is the nature of the injury in case of a sprain?

CHAPTER XXII.

THE CARE OF THE BONES.

How often we see young people stooping as they walk. The body bends forward, and the shoulders are drawn toward each other. This is too bad; because when the bones are young they may be bent easily, so that unless one is careful he will grow up narrow-chested and round-shouldered.

Shall we tell you how to have a fine, erect figure? Walk with the whole body erect, and the shoulders thrown well back. Later in life, when the bones become harder, you will not be able to walk easily in any other way.

Do you think it is a good practice to bend over your books while sitting at your desk; or to sit on one foot; or to take other awkward positions? When you are at home, did you ever notice how natural it is to slide down in an easy chair; or to bend over your sewing or reading? You certainly will not do any of these, if you only remember that when the bones are growing, they can have their shape changed. You can do much toward making yourself erect and graceful or stooping and unnatural. Which will you choose?

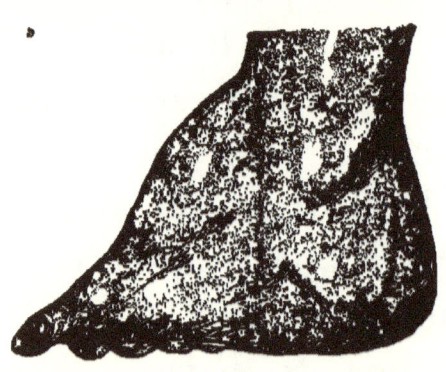

FIG. 29. The foot of a Chinese woman.

Do you think that Fig. 29 looks anything like a foot? Yet we made this sketch from the model of a foot of a Chinese woman. It illustrates what we have just said, — that it is possible to change the shape and position of bones.

Pressing the ribs too tightly about the waist injures the health. The clothing can be made to fit nicely and snugly, and yet not be tight enough to change the natural form. Do your shoes ever pinch your feet? They should not; for shoes are made to protect the feet and not to change their shape. High-heeled shoes cause in-growing toe nails, corns, and a great deal of discomfort.

Do you think Nature intended the heel of the foot should be a good way from the ground? Yet just think what high heels some people have to their boots! High heels give an awkward, stiff appearance to the walk, and cause a number of distressing complaints. We are sure our boys and girls like the "spring heels" best; while they will always use the "common sense" heels when they are older.

ALCOHOL AND TOBACCO.

Do you think the bones in our bodies are exactly like those we sometimes see on the ground? Oh, no! You know better than this. The bones on the ground are dead, while these in our bodies are alive and are full of blood vessels.

Do our bones grow larger and stronger as our bodies grow? Most certainly; and for this reason we should be very careful to take nothing that will check or harm their growth. Did you know that if alcohol be used while the bones are very young, they will not grow so fast nor so large?

But there is something else that affects the growth of the bones. Can you guess what it is? You will not have much trouble in guessing, if you know any young boys who have used cigarettes for some time. We hope you do not know any such; but if you do, we believe that you will nearly always find them smaller than other boys of the same age.

Boys, do you wish to grow to be large, strong men? Then, listen! You never can, if you use tobacco in any form. You will be shorter in stature, and your whole body will be poorly developed. To be sure, there may be some exceptions to this rule, but we believe the rule generally holds good. Shall we give you the rule again? Here it is:—

Boys who begin the use of cigarettes

at an early age, and keep up the habit for years, seldom reach their full growth.

Remember, boys, we are talking to you, not to the young man who has completed his growth. The effects of cigarettes on a young, growing body are much more serious than on a body which has reached its full growth. Knowing all these things, do you think you can afford to run the risk of trying a single cigarette?

TOBACCO STUNTS THE GROWTH.

QUESTIONS.

1. Describe the correct manner of walking.
2. What about the methods of sitting?
3. What does the deformed foot of a Chinese woman illustrate?
4. Why should the clothing not be tight around the waist?
5. Why not wear high-heeled shoes?
6. What is the difference between the bones in our bodies and those we may see on the ground?
7. What is said about the growth of the bones?
8. What effect may alcohol have on the growing bones?
9. Name something else that affects the growth of the bones.
10. What is said about the use of cigarettes?
11. What class of persons do cigarettes harm most?

CHAPTER XXIII.

THE BRAIN, SPINAL CORD, AND NERVES.

WAS not Nature very wise in placing the brain in such a well protected spot as the skull provides? Think how many

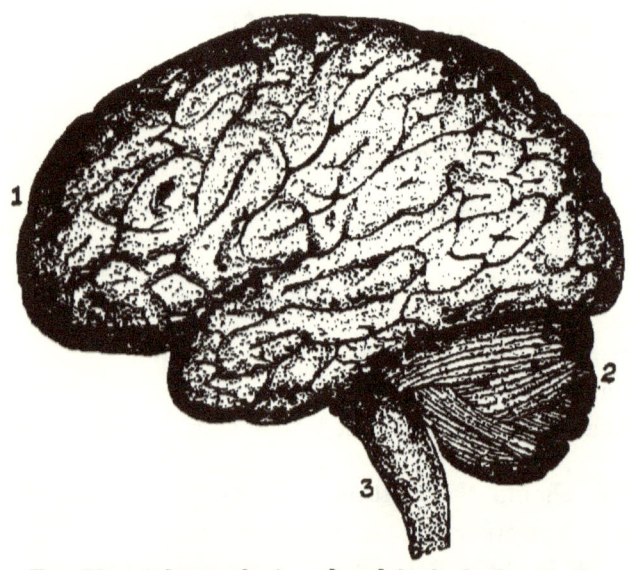

FIG. 30. A human brain. 1 and 2, the brain; 3, the beginning of the spinal cord.

hard knocks this strong box receives during an ordinary life! If these knocks fell directly on the brain they would completely destroy it; but within the skull it is quite safe. What is this brain for? Why, it is with the brain that you think and study. It is because of the brain that you can remember the things told you in this lesson.

Now use your brain, and tell what we said about muscle and exercise. Did we not tell you that the muscles were made strong by proper exercise? This is also true of the brain. Using the brain makes it stronger. How can we use it? By studying at school, by reading good books at home, and by keeping noble and kind thoughts in the mind. Shall we tell you something right here that will give you a great start in life? Always choose good books and good companions.

Does the heart work all the time? No, it rests a trifle after each beat. Do the lungs have any rest? Yes, they rest a short time after each breath. The brain and all parts of the body must have rest. Can you tell what brings rest to the whole body? Sleep. Without sleep a person cannot long remain in good health. Perhaps you are sleepy sometimes, are you? Do you think you could keep awake through a whole night? No, indeed; not if you are in good health.

How long would you like to sleep? Do you like to get up early in the morning? Shall we tell you how long you ought to sleep? Well, we cannot regulate this to suit each person. We can only say that the growing body needs a great deal of sleep. Each night should bring sleep, and plenty of it. But this we can tell you positively: the best time for sleep is in the early part of the night.

Go to bed early; and have quiet, restful sleep. Do not lie in bed after waking up in the morning. Get up early, and enjoy the most beautiful part of the day.

> "All the day do what is right,
> And sweet your sleep will be at night."

If you will look at Fig. 31, you will notice the brain at the upper part. Below

the brain is the spinal cord.   This goes
from the brain down the center of the
backbone.   Notice some
large nerves going to
the arms and the lower
limbs.   Smaller ones go
to the muscles and the
skin.

We have told you
nothing about the nerves
yet.   What are the nerves?
Suppose you prick the
end of your finger with a
needle!   That will tell
you.   How does the pain
get to your brain so you
know you are hurt?   In
just this way : The needle
touches a little nerve in
the end of the finger.   This
nerve sends the message
of pain up the arm until

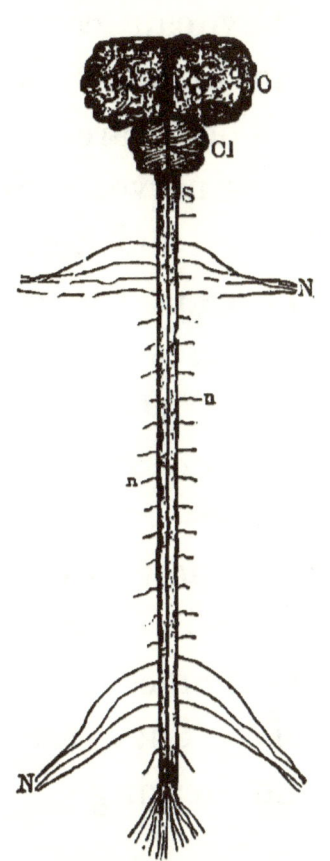

FIG. 31.   C and Cl are the
same as 1 and 2 in Fig. 30.   S
is the spinal cord ; N, N are the
large nerves which go to the arms
and lower limbs ; n, n are small
nerves which go to the skin.

it reaches the spinal cord, then the message
travels up the spinal cord to the brain.   So

now what are nerves for? They carry messages from one part of the body to another. They can carry many kinds of messages, and in many directions.

There are some strange things about these nerves. Some of them can do special things and nothing else. For instance, the nerves of the eyes can do nothing but carry messages of light from the eyes to the brain; and the nerves of the ears carry only messages of sound.

These special nerves give the senses. Do you know how many senses there are? We generally say there are five. Can you give the names of the senses so familiar to us all? They are sight, smell, taste, touch, and hearing.

ALCOHOL AND THE BRAIN.

Sometimes persons meet with dreadful injuries; yet, if they are in their right mind, they can be brave and bear the pain. But when the brain is harmed, so that the person does not know what he says and does, how much more sad it is!

We know of something that acts as a poison to the brain. It makes the brain stupid and dull. If enough of it be taken, it may affect the brain so that the person lies as if dead. Do you know the name of this poison? It is alcohol. When a person takes even a small quantity of alcohol, his brain begins to be affected by it. He talks in a foolish manner, and says things that his good sense would keep him from saying if he had not taken the alcohol.

Who can tell what a man will do when under the influence of strong drink? He may quarrel with his best friends without a cause. He is likely to be cruel to those whom he should love and care for, though he may be kind and tender when sober. Think what horrible deeds it leads men to commit, — deeds they would never do if they were not under the influence of something that had poisoned the brain.

Does a person have to be intoxicated in

order to have his brain harmed? No, indeed. Even small doses, long continued, often weaken the mind. A person who has a weak mind is not very likely to succeed in life. He cannot think or work well. His sense of right is dulled; and even if he sees what is right his will is so weak that he fails to act as he should.

A man frequently knows that he is ruining himself with alcoholic liquors, and he resolves that he will stop using them. But his appetite for alcoholic drinks is stronger than his will, and he keeps on drinking.

No one can afford to run the slightest risk of forming a habit that may result in such great injury.

TOBACCO AND THE BRAIN.

It is a sad fact that there are many young boys who are forming a habit that will harm their brain. Tobacco harms the brain, so that those boys who use it are generally the poorest students in the school.

Do you want to know where to find the boy who smokes? Well, never go to the head of the class for him. Look down toward the foot of the class. Tobacco so affects his brain that besides making him a poor scholar, it leads him to be deceitful and untruthful.

———

"The brain is the office;
  Each girl and each boy
  Has nerve lines that whisper
  Of sorrow and joy.

"Keep the brain office clean,
  The nerves steady and true,
  Or they cannot be fit
  For the work they must do."

QUESTIONS.

1. What is the brain for?
2. How can we make the brain stronger?
3. How can we use the brain?
4. Does the brain work all the time?
5. What brings rest to the whole body?
6. Where is the spinal cord?
7. Tell something about the nerves.

CHAPTER XXIV.

THE SENSE OF SIGHT.

DID you ever notice how well the eyes are protected? No harm can come to them from the back or from the sides. In fact, they are well surrounded by bone except in front, where the light enters.

Can you think of other ways in which the eyes are protected? Oh, yes, there are the eyelids. Notice how freely and quickly they can be moved. Of what use are those little delicate hairs, called the lashes, on the edges of the lids? They keep dust and insects from touching the eyeball.

Look one of your friends in the eye. Do you notice that round black spot? It is called the pupil. It is only a round hole. What is this for? In order that the light may pass into the eye.

Ask your friend to come to the window, where the light can fall on the eye. Look carefully now at this little pupil, and notice that it is getting smaller and smaller. Now have your friend cover his eye with his hand for a minute or two. Be ready to look quickly, as soon as he removes his hand. When he removes it, notice that the pupil is much larger.

From this we learn that when the light is bright the pupil is small, but when the light is dim the pupil is large. Did you ever see the pupil of the eye of a cat? When you get home notice, if you can, what a long narrow slit it is. But if you cover the eye for a moment, or take the cat into a darker room, the pupil becomes very large and round.

Have you ever seen a person who is blind? How sad is such a misfortune! Some of you may have been obliged to remain in a darkened room, because you had some trouble with your eyes. How you wished once more to be out in the bright daylight! Indeed, we hardly realize what a precious gift is the sense of sight.

Let us tell you of a few things that may aid you in preserving your eyes and in keeping them strong : If your eyes are red or inflamed, or if reading gives you the headache, or if any use of the eyes gives pain, you should consult a physician at once. Do not do such foolish things as squinting, trying to look cross-eyed, or turning the eyes in an unnatural way. Looking at bright lights, such as the sun or the electric lights, is also injurious.

If you should chance to get some dirt or dust into the eyes, some one may remove this for you by carefully wiping the eye with the folded corner of a soft handkerchief. Do not rub the eyes.

ALCOHOL AND TOBACCO.

It is a well known fact that alcohol, even in the lighter liquors, such as cider, beer, and wine, often injures the sense of sight.

Do you remember what we said about the red eyes of the hard drinker ? Sometimes they are so bad that they look bloodshot all the time. It is useless for such a person to ask the doctor to cure his eyes so long as he uses strong drink.

Tobacco smoke is bad for the eyes. It weakens and inflames them, and often makes the eyelids red along the edges.

Were you ever told there is a disease of the eyes, resulting in total blindness, which is caused by the use of tobacco? Such cases are rare, but they show the great power of the tobacco poison.

QUESTIONS.

1. How are the eyes protected?
2. Of what use are the eyelashes?
3. What is the round black spot in the eye called?
4. What is the pupil for?
5. When you come to the window, does the pupil become larger or smaller?
6. When the light is dim, is the pupil large or small?
7. Tell some things that may aid in preserving the eyes.
8. Does alcohol ever injure the sense of sight?
9. Is tobacco smoke good or bad for the eyes?
10. Does tobacco ever cause blindness?

CHAPTER XXV.

SMELL, TASTE, TOUCH, AND HEARING.

SMELL. Is not the odor from the apple orchard, when it is in full bloom, most delightful? And who does not enjoy the perfume of the rose? The sense of smell is useful to us in many ways. It enables us to enjoy many fruits and flowers. It also tells of the presence of things that are harmful to the body. Would you eat food that has a tainted smell? Would you like to breathe air in which there is a bad odor? No, indeed.

TASTE. Do you like the taste of olives? And did you, the first time you tried to eat them? How is it with tomatoes and oysters? Do you like them now, and were you always fond of them? Sometimes things which were disagreeable to us at first finally become very agreeable. Thus we learn that the sense of taste can be educated.

Tobacco greatly affects the taste. The tongue, and all the tissues around the mouth, become filled with the flavor of tobacco. This flavor remains in the mouth all the time, thus preventing the person from enjoying the true taste of anything.

TOUCH. We asked in the last chapter if you had ever seen a blind person. If so, did you see him read the Bible by passing his fingers over the letters that are only slightly raised from the page?

This shows how highly trained can be the sense of touch. This sense is in the skin, and extends over the whole body.

HEARING. Do you think the ear, which is on the side of the head, is all there is to the organ of hearing? No, indeed. The sense of hearing is deep in the bones back of the ear. The part you call the ear is of use only to catch the sound and send it along a canal to the deeper parts.

It is a great misfortune to lose the hearing, yet how careless many persons are about preserving it! You should not clean the ears with a pin, nor with any other hard substance. By failing to observe this rule trouble is often caused, which results in a gradual failing of the hearing.

Did you ever speak loudly in any one's ear? You certainly will never do it again, after you learn that it might cause deafness. Blows on the ears are always dangerous. You should not allow cold air to blow in your ears; it often causes a cold.

———•———

"Kindly we part! Love in each heart
To God, who happiness gives!
Singing His praise, we 'll walk in His ways,
And serve Him while each of us lives."

QUESTIONS.

1. Tell how the sense of smell is useful to us?
2. Give some illustrations showing how the sense of taste can be educated.
3. How does tobacco affect the taste?
4. Give an illustration showing how highly trained the sense of touch can be.
5. Is it wise to speak loudly in any one's ear? Why not?
6. Repeat the above verse.